By the same author

HEIRESS APPARENT

THE NIGHT OF THE PARTY

THE UNFORGOTTEN

FRANCESCA

DARK SYMMETRY

DARK SYMMETRY

Laura Conway

Saturday Review Press / E. P. Dutton & Co., Inc.

New York

First American edition 1973

Library of Congress Catalog Card Number: 73-78647
ISBN 0-8415-0270-6
PRINTED IN THE UNITED STATES OF AMERICA

DARK SYMMETRY

Prologue

She had been far away, wandering in a world which, at first strange and vaguely terrifying, had become familiar to her, because she had stayed there for uncomprehended ages. There was no way by which she could measure Time, other than by experience, and it seemed to her that she had now touched every spiritual experience. She had known utter joy and unbelievable desolation. She had been in the close company of the one who was dearest to her, and had yet been blessedly free. She had been lifted into the serenity of the clouds, and pitched into the blackness of a foul nightmare. And then she had known she was alone, for the first time in her life, for that other one had left her. She was sad, she was even aghast, for, though she had often longed for freedom, she realized that now it was hers she would find it a difficult possession. She would not know what to do with it. All was darkness; she could not see an inch ahead of her, and she was aware of the uselessness of striving for herself. She must drift with the tide, and that was pleasant enough. So she gave herself up to the force which was driving her back to life.

There was an immense fatigue. There was warmth and the softness of the bed beneath her. There was the golden glow of the sun which fell upon her face—she knew it was golden, even though her eyes were closed; there was the taste of the food which was slowly spooned into her mouth, and the conscious motion of swallowing it. Each sensation was separate and clearly realized. Last of all came sound. She listened to the voices which spoke to her, as the two people, one of whom was a stranger, though the other she remembered, stood on either side of her bed.

'It's quite certain now, isn't it? The operation is a success,' said the woman's voice which she knew.

'An emphatic success,' replied the unknown man. 'But once Courser said there was a chance, I had every confidence.'

'She will owe him more than her life,' the woman said. 'For there was no life for her before, the poor child. Thank God she is young enough to start over again.'

'That certainly is a cause for thankfulness. She is not yet twenty-two, I think you said.'

'Twenty-two in November. Three weeks to go. But she's as ignorant of ordinary life as a child of seven or eight. She was kept so apart, they both were. That was their mother's wish, the best thing really. They were so handicapped, and Mrs Norman was determined that the world should never find them out. Well, she had sufficient money . . . it would have been impossible without that, and as it was, I and the two servants gave our solemn promise that we would never speak of it, never allow it to be guessed outside . . .'

'And the girls submitted?'

'What else could they do? They never knew an outside life. I was their governess, but I had to be careful what I taught them. Of course they had to know they were different, but Monica, I am sure, never minded. Marcia was different; so dominated, so suppressed, and so lovely.'

'That is often the way, I believe. Dispositions in such cases vary. This girl, Marcia, is the more sensitive, the more talented?'

'Definitely so. She is artistic . . . she paints well, she has a lovely singing voice, she has a great liking for verse, for music . . . and the other hated all that, and was jealous because Marcia's tastes were different. It was rather dreadful, Doctor, that possessive affection . . . and then their poor mother . . .'

'She never reconciled herself to it, I understand.'

'No—but she was a good woman. She did her best, though it was a sore trial to her. She tried to think of them as ordinary children, but she could never bring herself to show them affection, though she tried. I have seen her kiss them, make herself fondle one or other of them, and all the time with a sick expression, a sense of shuddering horror.'

'Poor soul.'

'Don't think I judge her for it, Doctor. *I* could love them both, though it was this one who meant most, far the most to me, but it might have been different if I had borne them. I can't tell.'

'You must be prepared for the great shock it will be to Marcia when she knows she has lost both her mother and her sister. Her health, her bodily health, will be as good as ever, but her mentality—well, nobody can say how that will be affected—not yet.'

'I'm not afraid,' the woman said. 'I love her . . . I will look after her, while she needs me. And then there is the money. It will be all hers now, and everything in the world is open to her. She can travel, make new friends, lead a normal life, and I suppose she can marry.'

'There is no reason why she should not.'

There was a pause and then the woman said, 'Will it be noticeable?'

'The effect of the operation? Certainly not. There may be a slight scar, but not more than the scar caused by any operation.'

With a deep sigh the woman said, 'How thankful I am we lived in such seclusion. Nobody knew anything about the family. Both the maids were devoted to Mrs Norman. They were old and had been in her service before her marriage. They believed it would be a sin to break their solemn vow of secrecy. Besides, she had promised to provide for them, and she has. Nobody saw them. When we had to have a gardener in, which was seldom, for the greater part of the grounds were completely overrun, the girls were kept out of the way. When there were necessary repairs to the house, they and I stayed in whichever wing needed nothing done to it. Mrs Norman had no near relatives and never entertained. It was a bleak, tragic life for her, for she had been a well-known society girl years ago. Her husband left her before the children were born. I don't know why—only the bare fact. Well, I dare say she was a trying woman to live with. She must always have been remote and cold . . . too cold for marriage.'

'Is the father still alive?' the doctor asked.

'I have no idea. She never spoke of him and there was no mention of him in her will. Apart from the legacies left to the servants and to me, Marcia inherits everything.'

'Then all sets fair for her, and she starts with a clean slate,' said the doctor.

The voices drifted away. The girl heard their retreating footsteps. She had not yet opened her eyes, she did not want to open them. In darkness it was easier to think. The vista which was spread before her was enormous. She could not thoroughly envisage it, but then how could that be expected of her? It was true, as Janet had said, that she had less experience of the world than a child of seven. She had only known in a theoretical way that there was an outside world, which she had believed was to be for ever barred to her. She had, she supposed, thought of her situation romantically. She was the imprisoned princess, who would spend her life in solitude, trying to content herself with books of poetry, with the companionship of the few people who surrounded her, with her sister's love.

Quite consciously she had done her utmost to idealize Monica, had insisted to herself that that possessive love was noble and wonderful. Monica, she was sure, had never been swayed by such feelings as sometimes swayed her . . . a terrible impatience and disgust. A longing to be alone, a fearful rebellion which thrust its way through the enchanted princess fantasy.

And now that bondage was over, but in the first full knowledge of it, she felt no relief, only an overwhelming sense of loss. Tears trickled from beneath her closed lids and were on her cheeks when Janet Cameron re-entered the room.

'Why, darling,' said the soft Scottish voice. 'There's nothing to cry about . . . turn over, and forget the dream which hurts you.'

Then at last Marcia opened her eyes. Deep grey eyes which looked grievingly into Janet's blue ones. 'I wasn't asleep, Janet. I heard,' she said.

'Oh, my dear!' Janet's thin arms went out to encircle her, and pressed her close to her flat bosom. 'Why was I so incautious? But then we've been talking over your head for this long while past, and you didn't hear a word of it.'

'How long?'

'It's over seven weeks ago that you were brought here, darling. Do you remember anything of what happened?'

Marcia nodded. 'Oh, yes . . . I remember the landslide. I remember walking in the cliff garden and Mamma was with us . . . she wasn't often, as you know; and then suddenly there was the crumbling of the earth and we fell . . . fell.'

'Don't think of it,' Janet begged.

Marcia sighed against her breast. She said, 'Did they both—at once . . .?'

'Yes. The doctors say it must have been immediate. They were terribly crushed, and you . . . well, at first we thought you were gone too, but you moved a bit, and then you were brought here.'

'Here!'

'You're in a nursing home, darling. You've had the finest attention. The operation was performed by Mr Courser. He's the most famous surgeon known today, a pioneer, people call him. There were other operations afterwards, five in all. The last one was a fortnight ago, but from the first he was sure you would live . . .'

'Am I . . . am I . . .?' Marcia's voice broke on the questions she could not utter.

'Now, then,' reproved Janet tenderly. 'You heard what the doctor said; you must have, if you heard all the rest.'

'Yes, I heard,' Marcia agreed, 'but it's hard to believe. Can I really be the same as any other girl?'

'Exactly the same. You heard him say how it would be —a clean slate.'

Marcia clung to her, shaken by heavy sobbing. 'Need I go back there again—to that house?'

'Never, unless you want to. It's yours to live in or to sell. Everything is yours. You are a very fortunate girl. God has been good to you.'

'But not to them—not to Monica.'

'Yes, good to them too,' Janet said firmly. 'They're at rest, and likely your Mamma is taking a different view of

Monica now.'

'They are together, Janet, but I am alone . . . terribly alone. It's wicked of me to be glad, and in a way I'm not . . . I shall never forget, I shall always miss her . . . but still I'm glad.'

'And very natural too. You would never have had a real life, if poor Monica had lived. I wouldn't say it then, but I can now.'

Marcia's wet cheek was pressed close to her own. Satin smooth it was, thought Janet, and always had been, for Marcia had been blessed with a lovely skin and a lovely face and body.

'Oh, Janet, don't leave me, ever,' Marcia entreated.

'Never, while you want me.'

'I shall always want you. I love you, and you will always be the one who will understand.'

I

Alma Walters read her son's letter for the third time and wondered distractedly what she could possibly do about it. Nothing, of course, since the marriage had taken place about two days ago. The very suddenness and secrecy of it dismayed Alma, and surely, she thought, was sufficient reason for blaming Louis. It was not like him to be either impulsive or secretive, but in this case he had been both. The unknown girl must have bewitched him, she thought, and as she did so, a curious shiver rippled down her spine.

Now, she thought, she knew the reason for the black depression in which she had been immersed for the last few days. It had terrified her, for this horrible miasma of the spirit had come upon her before, when ill threatened those whom she loved.

Alma sighed. She had never been a possessive mother, had never tried to influence Louis unduly, or at least not since he had reached manhood. At thirty he certainly had the right to choose for himself. Financially he was independent of her. If they shared the same home, that was chiefly for her sake, as she realized. Louis had been happy to live with her, and would have continued to do so while he was unmarried, though his work sometimes took him away from Devonshire for long periods; but he could easily have lived elsewhere. The fact that they were devoted companions had been her joy and pride, but she had always known that in the nature of things this was not likely to continue indefinitely.

She had been glad, sincerely glad when Louis had evinced such an interest in Antonia Benham. Dear, sweet, reliable Toni, whom they had known for years, though for the last three years she had been living with an aunt in New York. But six months ago she had returned to her father and to the young stepmother, whose advent had been the indirect cause of her leaving home. However, three years had done something to mellow Stella Benham, that and her husband's illness. She had been charmed to welcome her grown-up stepdaughter, whose existence had once seemed a drawback. Toni was a trained nurse, therefore nobody could be a more desirable companion for a sick man.

Alma had not wondered at the fact that Louis had been so attracted to Toni; for attracted he had been, she would never believe otherwise. But then he had suddenly decided that Madrid must be the setting for his new book, and as he had never been to Spain, he decided to spend a month there.

In Madrid, according to the letter which Alma had read for the third time, he had met this girl, Marcia Norman. They had stayed at the same hotel, and then, when the month was up, Marcia and the companion, who appeared to act as her chaperon, had returned with Louis and they had been married in London two days ago by special licence.

But why the secrecy, and why the haste? Why hadn't Louis asked her to the wedding? She could have joined him in London at only a few hours' notice. But the normal, the decent thing would have been to have brought the girl to stay here, and to have married her after a reasonable interval.

Perhaps, however, he had thought of Toni. Alma had not the slightest idea of how far things had gone with them. She did not suppose Louis had actually asked Toni to marry him, but she must have expected that he would on his return. He had written to her, two or three times, but only in the first weeks of his absence.

Alma sighed heavily and pushed the letter into the pocket of her cotton frock. Louis had said that he would be driving down with his bride and Miss Cameron, her companion. This meant there would be much to do. Shopping in Seacrest--beds to prepare and, if possible, extra help must be obtained. Hetty, her young maid, could scarcely cope with such an unexpected influx, and Louis, as she knew, would be worried if he thought he had put fresh work upon her.

The house was roomy, and although Alma was not exactly house-proud (she owned three beloved spaniels who were welcome to roam as they would, and too often left signs of their presence in the way of muddy paws on the carpets and the polished floors) she could not tolerate any sign of neglect.

There was plenty to do before the evening meal, by which time they would all have arrived, but nevertheless Alma lingered in her rose garden. She had received a shock and the cool, silent beauty of the garden was soothing. She had a sense of being remote from the pressure of life as she absently snipped off dead blooms, and picked a handful of half-opened ones with which to decorate the rooms.

But at last she gathered up her flowers and moved towards the house, and as she did so drew in her breath with a sigh of distress, for a small, slight figure was approaching her down one of the winding paths, and almost instantly she came face to face with Toni Benham, looking as fresh as a rose, Alma thought sadly, in her pink cotton dress.

She was twenty-five, and a small, dark slip of a girl, not exactly pretty. Her brown skin was clear and her dark hair glossy and thick. She had intelligent, sympathetic hazel eyes, but her features were unremarkable, though her quick smile was charming. Alma loved her, and loved her looks, because they were, she thought, the fitting exterior for a loyal, brave and proud personality.

'I came over to beg a lettuce,' Toni said. 'I put down some new ones last week, but the old ones have all bolted, I don't know what went wrong. I'm afraid I'm not much of a gardener.'

'You haven't time to be,' Alma said, walking with her towards the house. 'Come in and have a cup of coffee, and I'll pick you as many lettuces as you want afterwards.'

'Coffee? Isn't it rather early for that?' Toni said. 'It's not quite ten o'clock.' And then she added quickly, 'At least it's early if you have had your breakfast—but I don't believe you have.'

'I didn't want any,' Alma said.

'Oh, really, that's too bad,' Toni said with concern. 'And I expect you've been up since eight.'

'Yes, I got up when I heard the postman.'

This was said deliberately in order to elicit the obvious question. But Toni hesitated a moment before she asked, 'Any news of Louis?'

'Yes, I'll tell you when we have had our coffee.'

They went into the house through long french windows which opened into the dining-room. Though Toni was often at Meadow House, she never failed to give it a deep and satisfied admiration, when she had leisure to look around. In its quiet way it claimed attention, made one wonder wherein lay its complete satisfaction, for of course there were flaws. Alma was not a particularly wealthy woman and the yellow linen curtains were slightly faded by the sun, and some of the rugs which covered the polished floor were definitely shabby. The furniture however, was beautiful, dark old oak, and the proportions of the room delightful. There was an ingle-nook fireplace, and windows looking out upon the garden which was Alma's chief pleasure.

It was a home, thought Toni wistfully, very conscious that the house where she now lived with her father and stepmother was anything but. That was a much grander house, adequately staffed, but it had none of the character and warmth and restfulness which characterized Meadow House.

On the mantelpiece there was a photograph of Louis, and Toni walked over and gazed at it. It was a good likeness which had been taken only a few months ago, when his publishers had requested a new portrait for the jacket of his latest novel. His women fans would be delighted with this photograph, for it would typify their ideal of a successful novelist. Louis, Toni considered, was not handsome, but he had many good points. He was a big man and well made. He had blunt features and a square chin, and eyes which were kind and often amused, and a mouth which was uncompromisingly firm. In his photograph he was lying back in a deck chair, smoking, a book on his knee. He could not have looked lazier.

Toni was still standing before the photograph when Alma re-entered, followed by a maid, with the tray which held the coffee pot, cups and saucers and biscuits.

'Come and have your coffee, child,' said Alma.

Toni obediently took the cup which was handed to her, but refused a biscuit, explaining that she had eaten a huge breakfast only an hour previously. She glanced at Alma with her first premonition of pain, for it was plain to see that Alma was troubled. She was pale, and she looked distinctly older than usual. A slender, upright woman, with delicate features, crowned by soft, grey hair which curled all over her head. As a rule there was something elusively young about Alma, but today she looked worn and even severe. Toni put down her cup and said, 'There's something the matter. May I know what it is?'

'You will have to know, my dear. Everyone will know. I can't deny that it's a blow to me.'

In her heart she added, 'And a blow to you, too, my poor Toni, though I must pretend not to know that.'

'Is anything wrong with Louis?' Toni asked.

Her voice was calm. Alma was not surprised that she got up and moved over to the window, where she stood looking out on the garden, her back half-turned.

This made it easier for Alma, and she said, not knowing how to soften the blow, 'Oh, no, nothing at all . . . except that I find it very hard to understand why he has done this thing, at least in such a furtive way. He is coming home today, and—oh, Toni, he is married.'

There was an instant of complete silence. To Toni it was as though Alma's last words had been uttered in a booming voice which might have been heard at the uttermost ends of the earth. 'He is married . . . he is married!' But it couldn't be true, argued her stunned mind. How could Louis be married, when he loved her? She was positive about that, recalling, in a split second of time, their last meeting. She had been out when he had called at her father's house to say goodbye, and had only returned ten minutes before he had to leave to catch his train for London. But he had managed to dislodge her from the others and had steered her into the garden. It had all been rushed and confused, but Toni would never forget the tenderness in his eyes as he held her hands and said, 'I was counting on this last afternoon together. I've so much to say to you. I've been trying to say it for weeks . . . but somehow it never seemed the right moment. And now there isn't time—but I shall say it when I come back. Meanwhile I can write to you—and don't forget me, dear.'

She had laughed softly, though her heart was hurt because she had been cheated.

'I could scarcely forget anyone in a month,' she had said. 'Certainly not you.'

He had not attempted to kiss her, but he had pressed her hands hard, before he released them, and she had stood by the gate watching him as he walked away.

From Spain he had written to her. Two long, friendly letters, with a hint of something deeper than friendliness, or so she had believed. He had said in one letter that it would be wonderful if she could have been with him in Madrid, and in the second letter he had told her that he had been looking round to try to find something to bring home for her, but that for a precious person it was difficult to hit upon anything truly suitable. After that second letter there was a long interval, and then about a fortnight ago she had received a postcard of the Alhambra, with a scrawled line on the back of it, which could certainly have been written to anyone.

It seemed to Toni that it was at least a quarter of an hour before she found her voice, but in fact it was no more than a minute. 'But . . . when?'

'Two days ago, by special licence in London. His wife was a Miss Norman, Marcia Norman. He met her in Spain. I know no more than that, my dear.'

For a moment Toni could not force herself to speak. She stood in the same position, not looking at Alma. At last she said, 'Louis is not usually impulsive.'

He had not been impulsive so far as she was concerned. They had known each other all their lives, though their friendship had been interrupted by the three years which she had spent in America; possibly those three years had given her something, a freshness, a novelty which had briefly attracted Louis, had made him believe that he loved her.

'I can't help feeling,' said Alma, 'that there's something unnatural about it.'

Toni turned then, touched by the woe in the other's voice, and momentarily forgetting herself. 'Oh no, darling,' she said. 'Why should there be? People do fall quickly in love.'

'Yes—but why this immense hurry? He could have become engaged, and brought her home to see me. Then, if they both wanted only a short engagement, they could have been married here . . . or—or anywhere else; at her parents' house, if she has parents.' Tears sprang to her eyes, and fell slowly down her cheeks. Toni, in all the years she had known Alma, had never seen her weep, and she was shaken by pity. She put her arms round her.

'Oh, Toni, I love him so, and I'm afraid,' Alma faltered.

'But, darling, he's a man, he can look after himself.'

'There's scarcely a man in the world—any nice man—who can look after himself. I've been so depressed these last days. It was as though I was walking through a fog. I might have known something was wrong.'

'Alma, we have no reason in the world to think this is

wrong for Louis.'

'I'm not saying anything about reason . . . I wish I didn't have these horrible premonitions, for they are nearly always justified. You know they are.'

Toni, holding her close, could find nothing to say. It was true enough that Alma did on occasion appear to possess some psychic gift which warned her of trouble. Years ago her husband had been in a train crash, and Alma had been sick and ill throughout the day of the accident. Happily he had not been fatally hurt, but his injuries had been sufficiently alarming. Once when Louis had been far away from her, he had been seriously ill with pneumonia, and although Alma had received no news of this until he was on the road to recovery, the same sense of bewildered darkness had seized her.

'It's just the shock,' Toni said.

With the girl's kind arms round her, Alma nearly said, 'Oh, if only it had been you.' But she realized that this would be a serious blunder. Toni would be humiliated by any hints that Alma guessed how it was with her. Now, though they loved one another, or rather because they loved one another, they must both keep up this face-saving pretence.

'Why, oh why, do people give way to sudden infatuations?' Alma wailed. 'Marriage shouldn't be built on such a foundation. The happiest ones are nearly always between those who have tastes in common.'

'I don't think that naturally follows,' Toni objected. 'I can quite imagine that two people, destined for one another, might know it immediately they met, and be perfectly sure their lives would be incomplete without each other. Alma dear, shouldn't we hope this has happened in Louis's case?'

'I can't hope it . . . I'm sure it isn't so. But there's nothing we can do, Toni. I know I must put the—the apprehension I feel into the background, and greet this girl normally and try to like her. That's the conventional way to act, and I am—outwardly—a conventional woman.'

She moved out of the circle of Toni's arms, and going

over to the table, poured herself another cup of coffee. The liquid was only half-warm now, and must, Toni thought, be horrible, but Alma swallowed it thirstily.

'I shall have to drive into Seacrest,' she said. 'A really good dinner will make things easier. Gregg's may have some salmon. It's a ridiculous price, but a mayonnaise on this hot evening would be nicer than anything else. And there are raspberries ripening in the garden . . .'

She was now speaking vaguely and rather incoherently, and the intense expression in her eyes, which Toni thought of as her 'seer expression', had vanished. Suddenly Toni was conscious of an overwhelming weariness. She longed to get home, to be alone in her room, where nobody would see her and where she need make no effort to hide her sick pain.

'I must go back, Alma dear,' she said.

Alma looked at her vaguely. 'Yes, of course, but first you must have that lettuce.'

What an anti-climax! Toni could have laughed hysterically. Instead, she followed her out of the house to the vegetable garden.

Sympathetic to Toni though Alma was, she was glad to be alone, as she drove the pony-cart into the nearest town, which was some miles away. It was a relief to have broken the news, and she thought tenderly of Toni who had taken what must have been a shattering blow with such courage. She knew she was selfish because it was a comfort to know that Toni could not leave the district, because of her father's precarious state of health.

Edward Benham had had a stroke over a year ago, and had not been expected to recover. But to some extent he had, though he would always be an invalid, dependent and more or less helpless.

It was his good fortune that Toni was a trained nurse and loved him dearly. Until his second marriage they had been everything to each other, and it had been a blow to Toni when he had married a girl only three years older than herself. Stella Chase had been a Seacrest girl, the daughter of an unsuccessful lawyer with a large family.

Stella had been only too delighted to get away from the poverty-stricken conditions of her own home, even though in order to do so she had married a man twice her age. But she had been exceedingly jealous of Toni who, having trained as a nurse, had given up her hospital work to act as housekeeper to her father. It was because of Stella that Toni had accepted her aunt's invitation to spend a prolonged holiday with her in America, and eventually she had settled there for three years, only returning to take charge of her father, after receiving a letter of frantic appeal from Stella.

She was the best girl in the world, thought Alma, so loving and with such a strong sense of duty, that it was easy to impose on her. Marriage with Louis would have been the ideal solution to her difficulties, for she would have been near enough to her father to see him frequently, even if Stella had engaged a trained nurse. But now it seemed that Toni's bondage of love was to be indefinite, and as for Louis . . .

The soft warm air fanned Alma's cheeks, as she drove along the country lanes, and gradually her spirit became more tranquil. The black cloud of depression, which had made life hateful to her for the past few days, lifted, and her nerves steadied. For good or ill this marriage was now an accomplished fact; she could do nothing about it, except to make the best of it.

Alma had loved her own husband devotedly. On his death, seven years previously, she had believed that her heart was broken, but Time, she mused, dimmed all grief, however intense. Also there had still been much left in life to make her happy. Louis was her pride and joy. At school and at college he had been considered brilliant, and before his father died he had already published his first book. Since then he had worked assiduously, publishing a book a year. Because of his original outlook, his wide sympathies, and his fertile imagination, he had from the first made a success. The large sales of his books had at first surprised him, in exactly the same way as they still surprised Alma, but now Louis had become accustomed to success. He had something, he supposed, though he could scarcely have said what, which he managed to get into his work and which appealed to people of all types and creeds. He was quite simple and modest about this phenomenon and merely said he was lucky. Alma, of course, secretly considered him a genius, but she would never have dared apply such a word to him in his hearing, for he would have laughed in derision.

As the memory of her black mood receded, she endeavoured to view his marriage with optimism. There must be something remarkable about a girl who had so quickly ousted Toni from his memory. In any case, Alma had no intention of severing herself from her beloved son which she would if she failed in the warmth of her welcome.

The rest of the morning passed swiftly. She bought salmon and a large and expensive iced cake, and a fat pot of cream from the dairy. When she drove back to Meadow House there was plenty to be done. The first thing was to interview Hetty, to tell her that 'Mr Louis' was married, and to ask her if her elder sister Gladys, who was a widow with one child, would come up to Meadow House for a few hours each day and help with the housework.

Alma scarcely supposed she would be required for longer. No doubt Louis and his wife would want their own home. Louis might buy a house in the neighbourhood, or he might prefer to live in London.

The afternoon passed slowly. Alma picked flowers and massed them in tall vases and in a bowl for the centre of the dining-table. She cooked the salmon and, when it cooled, she contrived a really ravishing salad from vegetables grown in the garden. Raspberries were picked and chilled for desert. The big iced cake would make its appearance with the coffee.

She tried to rest for an hour, but although she stretched out her body in a long chair, her mind was feverishly active. She had heard that a review of the past frequently flashed across the memory of one who was about to die. Well, she did not suppose that she was in danger of immediate death, but nevertheless pictures of Louis in all stages of his development processioned through her mind. Though she might close her eyes, she could not shut out the vision of him in his babyhood, his little boyhood, his eager youth, his first adult success.

Hetty brought her a tea tray and she tried to eat, and was grateful for the refreshing tea. Soon afterwards it was time to go upstairs and dress. She looked into the room which had been prepared for Louis and his bride and could find no fault with it. It was a large, pleasant room with the light wood furniture becoming popular now at the beginning of the century. This room had hitherto been allotted to guests, but Louis's own room, which ran across the top of the house, and had sloping roofs and a dormer window, was not suitable for two people, though Louis liked it, because it had been his from boyhood days.

Carefully Alma selected her prettiest dress to wear. It was a pale grey gauze with a foundation of rose pink taffeta. The sleeves were long, but the bodice was cut in a deep V. The skirt was long and slim. Nothing could have suited Alma better with her small, elfin-pointed face, and her silver grey curls. Presently she heard the sound of horse's hooves coming down the road, and saw the landau which had been sent to meet the train. She went down the stairs, her heart beating rapidly. By the time she was at the door, Louis had alighted, and he went to her and took her in his arms. For an instant the carriage and its occupants were obscured to her.

'Mother darling,' Louis said, and there was penitent apology in the two words.

'I had your letter this morning,' was all Alma could find to say, but she clung to him.

'I know . . . it seemed better than a wire. I hoped it might be less of a shock.'

'I don't think it would be possible to minimize such a surprise,' Alma said, avoiding the word shock. 'But—but I wish you both happiness, my darling.'

As she spoke she slipped out of his arms, and moved towards the carriage. She saw three people. A lean, middle-aged woman still sitting in the back seat, a young and very beautiful fair girl, exquisitely dressed, who was evidently about to alight, a smaller, darker girl behind her.

Louis put his hand on Alma's arm and said, 'Darling,

this is Marcia, my wife . . . and this is Miss Cameron . . . Miss Janet Cameron.'

Alma scarcely heard him. Her fascinated gaze was fixed on the dark girl in the background. It was the fascination of repulsion, for she thought she had never seen a more sinister face. It was young, but it was evil . . . it was a dark face. A profusion of curly hair haloed it, the long eyes were set at a slightly slanting angle, the lips were very red and they smiled, a smile which was one of open and triumphant derision. She was dressed as Marcia was dressed, in white, so close to her that she seemed almost to melt into her.

A most dreadful sense of nausea swept over Alma. Her scalp tingled. She was icily cold to her feet. For a moment she could not speak, because her tongue had cloven to the roof of her mouth, but at last she stammered, 'But who—who is that?'

She realized that they were all looking at her in amazement, and Louis said, 'Mother, what is it? What is wrong?'

What could be wrong indeed? Alma brushed her hand across her eyes, as though a web or thickly meshed veil had fastened upon them. It cleared suddenly and she saw her new daughter-in-law very distinctly; saw that there was fear in her eyes, and that her lips were trembling.

Now there were only two people there besides herself and Louis. The girl with the dark face and the evil smile had vanished. Alma knew that in the flesh she had never been there at all. It was some creature from another world that she had seen, a being horrible and corrupt.

The ground shook beneath her feet, and the sky seemed to be closing down upon her. She murmured something indistinguishable and, before Louis could stretch out his arm to support her, she had dropped down on the ground, losing consciousness as she fell.

2

The evening meal was in progress. Alma sat at the head of the table and Louis sat at the foot. Marcia sat on Alma's right hand, and Janet Cameron on her left. Every now and again Louis glanced across the bowl of roses at his mother, and there was anxiety in his eyes, for although Alma smiled serenely and talked without apparent strain, it seemed to him that this evening for the first time he saw the signs of age upon her. Hitherto, apart from her silvery curls, Alma had looked extraordinarily youthful. Her small face was almost devoid of lines, her throat slim, and straight, and her body had the kind of soft bonelessness which is usually associated with youth. But now her skin had a slightly leaden tinge, her eyes were heavy, and it was obvious to him that, although she was carrying off the situation well, she was fighting exhaustion.

Her fainting fit had been of brief duration. She had revived almost as soon as he had gathered her up in his arms and carried her inside the house. It was the heat, she declared, and she had been rushing around all day making the necessary preparations for them. Besides, she owned, she had been terribly wrought up, for Louis's letter had been a shock, though that was not to say she didn't welcome with delight such a beautiful daughter-in-law.

It was prettily said, and Marcia who was herself white to the lips had tried to smile in return. But when Louis had taken her up to the room prepared for them, she had scarcely spoken a word. She was a silent person at all times, but now her speechlessness had a stunned quality, which scarcely surprised Louis, for it was certainly disconcerting to be received by a fainting mother-in-law.

But anxious and perplexed though he was, Louis, who was hungry, made an excellent meal. Janet also ate fairly well but Marcia and Alma merely played with the food upon their plates.

Alma was penitent when she observed her daughter-in-law's pale and downcast face, and she commended her because she was evidently making a great effort to respond to the remarks addressed to her. She was certainly a lovely girl, and looking at her Alma was scarcely surprised that Louis had plunged into a headlong romance which had ended in marriage.

Marcia was a slender creature of medium height, but although she probably weighed no more than eight stone she was pleasantly, seductively rounded. Her smooth arms were dimpled at the elbows, and a dimple also showed in her left cheek when she smiled. It seemed to Alma, who did not really want to love her, that there was everything lovable and endearing to be found in that oval face, with its delicate features, and large, dreamy eyes which were of a curious shade of misty violet. Dark golden hair fell in sculptured waves about a wide, high forehead and crowned a most noble little head set on a long throat. Her mouth was full and sweet and pensive, and Alma could imagine that when radiance lit her face and those lips parted in laughter, she was irresistible. Evidently she liked to wear white for she had arrived in a white linen suit and now wore a white silk dinner-dress. One arm was clasped by a magnificent diamond bracelet, which Alma doubted if Louis had given her, for it must have cost a great deal of money, and although he had done well with his books, he spent casually and easily and had not saved a great deal. But the ring on the third finger of Marcia's left hand he must have given her, for it was the conventional diamond solitaire.

Louis said, from his seat at the bottom of the table, 'You've been wonderfully patient, Mother, not to ask a single question about our marriage, especially as I gave you no information in my letter.'

Alma smiled. 'I thought you would find it less of an effort after a meal. And you did tell me you met Marcia in Spain, in the hotel where you were staying.'

Marcia said suddenly, 'I ought not to have let him, Mrs

Walters . . . it was too quick . . . I said so. It was different falling in love, we couldn't help that, but he doesn't know me well enough . . . only I was frightened. I've never lived by myself, or had to—to manage things, and when Janet told me . . .'

The girl's voice broke, it was trembling, and Alma fancied that there were tears beneath the protectively lowered lids. On impulse she put out her hand and covered Marcia's, which lay on the table near to her.

'Louis,' she said, 'is a man, not a boy. He knows his own mind. If he thought it best for you to be married immediately, then you need not blame yourself for letting him decide for you.'

'You're kind,' said Marcia in a low voice.

Nothing, thought Alma, could have been more disarming than that surprised gratitude. She felt Marcia's fingers twine about her own, and her resentment and pain were eased. The strange fear of the girl which had seized her and which she had fought against passed from her mind, and now she felt that she could indeed love Marcia.

Janet Cameron's voice broke the slight silence: 'We both overruled her,' she said. 'I was chiefly responsible, for I knew that when I told Louis, he would insist on marrying Marcia at once.'

'Told Louis what?' Alma asked, turning her gaze to the middle-aged woman, observing her more closely.

She was very thin and very plain, but it was a good face, thought Alma. There was strength and kindness in the pale blue eyes, and it was obvious that she adored Marcia.

'I am ill,' said Janet bluntly. 'I've been more or less ill for the last three months. Next week—the day after tomorrow actually, I am to go into a London hospital to have an operation . . . I should have gone before, but I couldn't leave Marcia. There were particular reasons why I couldn't. She has led a singularly sheltered life; until six months ago she had never left her home, and knew nothing of the world. But the pain has been bad lately and I knew the time would come when I couldn't look after Marcia, and so I told Louis what was wrong with me, and he insisted on an immediate marriage. In any case I am sure it would have been a short engagement, because, you see, they were both so passionately in love.'

She spoke with a stoic unconcern which forbade compassion. Alma sensed that there was a great deal which she didn't know, which perhaps she would never know, but Janet Cameron enlightened her to some extent.

'In that case,' she said, 'I am sure Louis and Marcia did the right and the wise thing.'

'I couldn't let Marcia stay around in hotels, miserable and lonely,' Louis said. 'Her home in Sussex was sold some months ago, after her mother was killed in an accident, and she has nobody else. Besides,' he added simply, 'I was only too glad to hurry on the marriage. I was afraid Marcia would stand out for a long engagement. It would have been natural if she had. She knew so little about me.'

'No—I knew everything,' Marcia said softly. 'From the very first minute that we met . . . then I knew.'

She raised her eyes and looked full at him with such a look of love and trust and tenderness, that Alma's last vestige of doubt left her. Louis got up and put his hand on his wife's shoulder and smiled at his mother.

'It's all right, you see,' he said.

Alma nodded. 'Yes, I see it is,' she agreed. 'I suppose that is really how love should be—immediate and irresistible.'

Marcia said, 'It was a kind of miracle. I couldn't believe it at first, but Janet said it was real. She said she knew that everything would be right for me, so that she could go into hospital with an easy mind.'

'You can do that, Miss Cameron,' Alma assured her. 'I am more sorry than I can say, about you, but Marcia's home is here, until Louis decides to take her away to another, and we will look after her. But we must think of you too, do all we can for you.'

Janet shook her head, saying brusquely, 'These is nothing you can do, except be good to her. She will reward you, it is her nature to be grateful. As for me—I am not young, and if I die tomorrow it would be no great tragedy. I hope none of you will worry about me. My surgeon is a Scot and an old friend. He will do his best for me.'

It was difficult to believe that she was speaking of her own imminent fate, for her manner was completely detached. Alma, who was sure that she, with a like danger threatening her, would be reduced to abject terror, regarded her with considerable respect. She said conventionally, 'I am sure he will, and when your operation is over and you can leave hospital, you will be able to come here and get thoroughly strong.'

Janet thanked her briefly, but Marcia's face was suddenly radiant with gratitude, and now she was indeed gloriously beautiful.

'Oh, Mrs Walters, thank you,' she said. 'I've been so worried, wondering, thinking that perhaps if Louis and I hadn't got a home by that time, we shouldn't be able to look after Janet.'

'This is your home, my dear, for as long as you want it, and any friend of yours will be welcome here,' Alma said, and then she added with a smile, 'Don't you think you could perhaps call me by my Christian name, as do other of my young friends—Toni Benham, for instance, who lives in the nearest house.'

She had not intended to mention Toni's name, on this first evening, and was annoyed with herself for the careless slip, as she saw the slight stiffening of Louis's expression, but Marcia said eagerly, 'I would love to . . . Please tell me about this Toni . . . is her home very near? Will she be my friend? I have never had a girl friend of my own.'

'Oh Marcia, you have met any amount of young people during the last six months,' Janet remonstrated.

'Yes, met them. But I have never had a friend to be intimate with. Just being friendly with people in hotels is different . . . but I've always wanted to run into another girl's house, and talk clothes with her and go shopping and be . . . be just ordinary . . .'

Once more her voice faltered and broke off, once more Alma was aware of mystery, and perhaps awareness showed in her expression, for Janet Cameron said briskly, 'If you are not too tired, Mrs Walters, could we have a little talk? Marcia has her unpacking to do, and then she should go to bed, for she is very tired.'

It was a peremptory request, and an odd thing, Alma thought, that now Marcia was married, Janet should still think it her business to direct her actions. But then she remembered that the marriage had only taken place three days ago. Janet had encouraged Marcia to marry Louis, but she had not entirely handed her over to him—as yet.

'Janet, my mother is tired too,' Louis expostulated.

'Yes, of course she is, but she may sleep better after we have had a talk. I can tell her more than you can tell her, and I have so very little time, as I must leave tomorrow.'

'Tomorrow?' Alma echoed. 'But I thought you said . . .'

'I am expected to be in hospital twenty-four hours before the time fixed for the operation.'

'I see. Then, in that case, of course I shall be only too glad to talk to you, Miss Cameron. Louis, suppose you show Marcia over the house and garden. Surely she can leave her unpacking until tomorrow.'

Louis opened his lips as though to protest, but then he thought better of it. He offered his hand to Marcia, who took it, and they went out together.

Alma nestled down into the cushions at one end of the settee, and Janet Cameron sat very upright in the other corner. Alma thought that she would have been more comfortable, more at ease, had she been occupied with some knitting. Those thin, strong, capable hands looked unnatural, clasped loosely in one another. Probably during Janet's fifty-odd years they had rarely been at rest.

'This, being the woman you are, must have been a very great shock to you,' Janet said, and for the first time her Scottish accent was noticeable. 'Before I met you I thought it might not much matter to you that your son had married so suddenly. It would have been better for you had you been a stronger, harder type.'

Alma smiled. 'I'm really quite tough. I've never had a serious illness in my life. My fragile appearance is deceptive.'

'But you fainted,' Janet said. 'That does not seem tough to me. I am critically ill, so they tell me, but even so I have never become unconscious, as you did.'

Alma said nothing. Her heart, she thought, had missed a beat, for Janet's words had brought vividly back to her the thing she had been trying to forget all evening.

'It was an exceptional occurrence,' she explained at last. 'As I told you, I had been rushing around all day and was overtired. Please, Miss Cameron, tell me everything about Marcia, which you think will help me to know her. She is a beautiful girl and she seems to be a sweet one.'

'You will never find a sweeter, but it would be useless for me to pretend that Marcia is an ordinary girl. She has led a queer, unnatural life.'

'Yes?' Alma's voice and expression were receptive.

Janet sat looking down at her loosely clasped hands. It was only with an effort that she prevented herself from clenching them together. The sharp pinprick of her nails biting into her flesh would have been a relief, but it was necessary for her to appear relaxed and at ease. Weeks ago Janet had decided just how much of Marcia's history she intended to reveal to Louis Walters and to his mother, and with Louis it had been easy. He was crazily in love and therefore very little interested in facts. He had asked no questions and had listened perfunctorily to Janet, when she had talked to him the night before the wedding. All he had wanted was Marcia, and he had wanted her as quickly as possible. But his mother was different. She was a nice woman, Janet thought, kind and sensitive, but it stood to reason that she wasn't prepared to accept a daughter-in-law from out of the blue, without apprehensive curiosity.

'I've known her from the time she was a tiny thing,' Janet said. 'I went to Mrs Norman when Marcia was no more than five, to be her governess. She was delicate, and Mrs Norman was delicate too, and lived a secluded life. She was an unhappy woman, poor thing, for her husband had left her before Marcia was born and she never seemed able to get over it.'

'Is he still alive?' Alma asked.

'That I couldn't tell you. Mrs Norman never spoke of him, and he certainly never came to the house all the years I was there. I don't know what their quarrel was. But she was eccentric, not a doubt of it. She had the child brought up in isolation, except for herself and me and the two servants. It was understandable at first, for Marcia was delicate, as I say, but she grew out of that, and then books and music, and so on, were not enough for her. But her mother would have it that way, and Marcia loved her and wasn't rebellious. She's not the sort to rebel. She lived in a dream, and only woke up from it when her mother was killed and she was free.'

'How was Mrs Norman killed?' Alma asked.

'It was a landslide. The house was set in acres of grounds, for Mrs Norman was a wealthy woman, and Marcia is wealthy too—everything was left to her. The grounds stretched right out to the cliff, and after a storm one day, she and Marcia were walking there, and the ground gave way under their feet . . .'

She gave a deep sigh and a shudder, and Alma said, 'What a terrible thing. Was Marcia badly hurt?'

'Yes, she was ill for months in a nursing home; there were bad injuries, but now she's as healthy a girl as you could find anywhere. She had a bad shock, of course, and even when she was fit to leave the nursing home, her nerves were not what they should have been. That's why I took her abroad, and it was quite time, too, that she should see something of the world.'

Alma asked incredulously, 'When you say that she and her mother lived in seclusion, do you mean that she literally saw nobody?'

'Well . . . practically . . . it was a lonely spot and Mrs Norman never asked a soul to the house. As for education, I did my best, but you might say that in many ways Marcia is not up to the standard of the other girls, though she's intelligent and a great reader.'

'If she reads, she will be educating herself all the time,' Alma said.

'That was her mother's attitude, though it was an old-fashioned one, for it seems to be the modern idea that a girl should have every possible experience whatever her station in life.'

'It all makes for character, I suppose. But I must admit—' and Alma smiled—'that it thrills me to know that my daughter-in-law has never been in love with anyone but Louis who will teach her all she needs to know of the world. That's as old-fashioned an attitude as her mother's, but I've noticed that most women when they reach middle age revert to old-fashioned ideas.'

'In love!' Janet seized on these words as though they shocked her. 'You can believe me, Mrs Walters, that Marcia knew nothing whatever about love until she met your son. I was a very strict chaperon when we started to travel around, and Marcia clung to me. She would never accept any invitation which did not include me. Now perhaps you can understand why it seemed so imperative that she should be married, in case things do not go too well with me.'

'Yes, of course I understand. You had a tremendous responsibility. Now it is Louis's, and I am sure he will consider it so.'

'He is a good man,' Janet said sombrely. 'It was the greatest relief when I saw how it was with them. I am not a religious person, but I had prayed that something of the kind might happen. From the first I liked Louis and knew he could be trusted. I encouraged them to get married at once, and I hoped she might be finding a real home and a friend in you—though that I had to take on chance.'

'I promise you I will be her friend,' Alma said.

Janet sighed. 'I know it . . . but there may be times when you feel she is a strange girl. I have given you only the merest outline of her history, but Marcia will tell you more, as she comes to know you better . . .'

She broke off as the door opened and Louis came in. He smiled at the two women and said, 'Marcia has gone off to bed, Janet, but she wanted to see you for a few minutes, while I talk to my mother.'

Janet got up at once and said good night to both of them. When Alma said she would see her to her room, Janet prevented her. There was no need, she assured her, she knew her way and had all she wanted.

'A brusque creature,' Alma said as the door closed upon her, 'but a good one. Louis, she has been very troubled about that child.'

'Well she might be,' Louis said, 'knowing how helpless Marcia was, and that there was a chance she might not live to protect her.'

'Is she very ill?' Alma asked.

He shrugged. 'I gather so, though she has told me little, and has made light of her illness to Marcia. It's a fact, I am sure, that she has scarcely given a thought to herself. She's a grand person, and I know she came first with Marcia, even when her mother was alive. I suppose she's been telling you something of her past life.'

'An outline. It's a queer story. The child seems to have been brought up as a nun. The mother must have been eccentric, to say the least of it. She made use of her wealth to seclude herself and Marcia from the world. Without money it would scarcely have been possible.'

'I wouldn't say that. If one desires solitude it is obtainable, even with very little money. There are few places more remote from the world than some of the cottages in the wilds of Scotland and Ireland. But, as you say, Mrs Norman must have been an eccentric, and a selfish one. She was most unfair to Marcia. That fantastic life might have continued for years, if her mother had not been killed.'

'Who was Mrs Norman?' Alma asked. 'Who was her husband?'

'That I can't tell you. I have her marriage certificate amongst a portfolio of papers which Janet handed over to me the other day. He is described as a journalist. Mrs Norman's father was an Australian. He made his money in that country, and increased it considerably by buying up property and re-selling it at a large profit when he eventually settled in England. He married an aristocratic Irish girl—her father was the younger son of a peer—but the family have died out. Marcia never saw either of her grandparents, in fact so far as she knows she has no relations.'

'You have an immense responsibility, Louis. Miss Cameron tells me that Marcia has a large fortune in her own right.'

'The capital is round about a hundred thousand, or so I

understand from Janet, who is the sole executor of Mrs Norman's Will. As I say, she handed all the papers over to me, but I'm no good at that sort of thing, and I shall leave everything in the hands of Marcia's solicitors. They are a reputable firm, in London. I did have the wit to make routine inquiries, as it struck me she was entirely at their mercy. Not that I need have worried, for Janet is a shrewd woman of business, and she would soon have taken all Marcia's affairs out of their hands, if she hadn't been entirely satisfied.'

Alma was silent for a minute and then she said, 'I suppose a great many people would think this important—I mean that you have married a girl with such a large fortune, but it doesn't seem important to me. In a way so much money is a complication.'

'It certainly is,' said Louis, and then he laughed. 'It's all the more complicated because Marcia has such original ideas. She wants to give it all away, but I feel that is going a bit too far.'

'What has given her such an idea?'

'Well you see until six months ago she had never been outside the grounds of her own home. Then, suddenly, she was shown the world as it is. One of the first things Janet did was to conduct her on a tour of London. She saw the West End and she saw the slums. Within the space of an hour she was made to realize the horrible inequality of life. Ever since she has been haunted by that glimpse of squalor and she can't understand how we can put up with it. In Spain she saw much the same thing, and before that, she had spent a fortnight in Ireland, which had been connected in her mind with beauty and poetry and Celtic legends. But once there, she saw a great deal which was neither poetic nor beautiful, for the Dublin slums were worse, I should think, even than those in East London. Now she hates her money, hates to think that she can have luxury, while others haven't even decency.'

'I must say I sympathize,' said Alma. 'Poor child, she is bound to have one shock after another.' She added thoughtfully, 'It would be a pity for her to become hardened, and yet unless she acquires some sort of protective skin she will suffer horribly. What do you intend to do about this? She will be guided by you, I suppose?'

She saw Louis's face soften; she saw mingled amusement and tenderness in his eyes. 'Yes, poor darling. She has a most exaggerated idea of my wisdom and humanity. Of course she must have her own will to some extent. But I have urged her to go slowly. If she intends to give half of her income away, she might as well have some fun out of it . . . see the results and be satisfied.'

'Oh Louis, that's a wise decision. I'm so glad,' Alma said.

Louis put his arm round her. 'You're the most unworldly woman, thank God. Darling, I've treated you badly . . . but I was afraid . . . I do adore Marcia, who wouldn't? She was like a lost child; absolutely terrified when she realized that Janet would have to go into hospital and perhaps be there for months. She hadn't the slightest idea how to look after herself, and anything might have happened to her. If I had been certain how you would react I would have brought her down here and given her over to you, and we could have married at leisure, but actually I had only one idea in my head—to safeguard her; to know that she was mine and that it was my business to look after her. You know in some ways she's not quite real to me; that's part of her fascination. Sometimes she makes me think of the old Celtic legends, about men who married faerie wives, and whose love for them made them human. Marcia is human enough in most ways though, thanks be.'

'I do understand,' Alma said, 'and I could be quite happy about it, if it wasn't for—for . . .'

She broke off, but Louis understood.

'You mean if it wasn't for Toni. Yes, I suppose I've behaved badly to her, but I never actually proposed to her, and I can't be sure how she felt about me.'

'I wondered how far it had gone,' Alma murmured.

'I couldn't say with certainty—not so far as Toni is concerned. We have always been the greatest friends, and I thought, before I left England, that it was more than friendship. I did say something vague to her on the day I left, but we only had a few minutes together. I asked her not to forget me, and she said she could scarcely do that in a month. Actually I'd planned that on my return I would ask her to marry me, but then I'd never been wildly in love with anyone. I liked Toni immensely, I admired her and was attracted to her. That was all, and within an hour of meeting Marcia I knew how little it was. It doesn't seem as though I have done Toni any harm, does it?'

'I hope not, dear.'

Louis looked at her with some alarm. 'She hasn't said anything to make you suppose . . .?'

'No, not a word. Only it was obvious to me before you left England that you were interested in her. Being prejudiced in your favour I thought that any woman would love you, if you loved her.'

He laughed. 'Oh darling, what absurdity!'

Alma was silent. She had her own ideas about Toni, but she knew it would be better for her if Louis could persuade himself that she had never thought of him as more than a friend.

Janet found Marcia sitting on the stool before her dressing-table mirror, brushing out her long, corn-coloured hair. It fell around her shoulders like a shining cape.

Marcia had unpacked a small case which contained necessities for the night and she was wearing a peach-coloured silk negligee which had been one of the first things she and Janet had bought after she had left the nursing home.

They had had a wonderful time, spending hours each day shopping—buying everything that could enhance Marcia's beauty. They had stayed at a famous hotel, had gone to theatres and concerts. To Marcia it had all been the sheerest magic, and in those days she had belonged wholly to Janet, was dependent on her, terrified of being separated from her.

Her marriage to Louis Walters had been eagerly abetted by Janet, but all the same, on this last night, it was impossible to repress nostalgic longings.

Marcia turned slightly as Janet stood behind her, and she said, 'Louis has a very happy home, hasn't he? If he hadn't met me it would have been enough for him.'

'I don't agree with that,' Janet said firmly. 'There comes a time when every man should marry. I have been talking to his mother, who is a nice woman. I am sure she would say the same.'

'I was—wondering about that talk,' Marcia said. 'Please tell me. Did you explain to her?'

'Partly—as much as she needs to have explained. She knows now that your upbringing was not ordinary. You won't have to worry about any mistakes you make, for she understands that you knew nothing of the world until six months ago.'

'But is that all? Didn't you tell her about—Monica?'

'I didn't mention her name. Neither Mrs Walters nor your husband knows that Monica existed.'

Marcia got up from her dressing stool, and thrust back her falling hair. 'But why? You made me promise not to mention her to anyone, not even to Louis, until you gave me leave. But I never understood . . . I mean I could just have said I had a sister. I'm not happy about it, Janet. I'm deceiving Louis—and it makes her angry too.'

'Now, Marcia!' Janet said warningly.

The girl's head drooped. 'I know you don't like me to say that sort of thing.'

'I most certainly do not. Monica has no longer the power to be pleased or angry. She has gone far away, and cannot influence your life any further. You must forget her.'

'And go on alone?'

'Not alone, you have your husband.'

'I love Louis,' said Marcia slowly. 'It's wonderful the way I love him . . . a thousand times more than I ever loved her, but he's not so close as she was . . . he's not exactly part of myself.'

'You don't want anyone to be a part of yourself. You are a separate individual. Near and dear though your husband may be to you, you must, like everyone else in the world, stand alone.'

'It's what I wanted—what I used to dream of, but it's so hard,' Marcia said. 'She doesn't want to be alone either. I think it's as you say, Janet: we were meant to separate, to lead different lives, but Monica won't, she . . . she tries to get back to me, and sometimes she does. This afternoon she was so close to me, almost as she used to be, though I couldn't see her, and that made her angry. All the way in the carriage she was pressing herself between me and Louis. I felt I had to edge up against the door to make room for her.'

'Marcia!'

'Janet, I know you say it's imagination, but I can't make myself believe it is.'

'You must discipline yourself. Tell yourself every time that feeling comes to you, that it is a wrong feeling. Monica is gone, and she is at peace.'

'Oh, I do hope so. I feel a traitor though, for not telling people about her. It's as though I tried to pretend she had never existed, almost as though I piled the earth on her, and stamped on it.'

'Oh, my darling.' Janet's voice was pitiful. 'Come sit down here beside me, and let us talk. We only have a little time. Tomorrow I shall be gone before you are up—no, don't protest, Marcia, that is how I want it to be. It's sad to say goodbye, and if all goes well, I shall soon see you again. Louis will bring you to see me in hospital. You know he promised. Now let us get this straight in our minds. Neither you nor I will ever forget Monica. You loved her and I pitied her. I always felt she was not really to blame for her disposition. The reason I didn't tell Mrs Walters or Louis of her existence, and made you promise to do the same, was to spare you. If once they knew she had lived and died when your mother died, there would be questions which you would find it hard to answer. It would make it impossible for you to put her out of your mind, it would intensify this fancy of yours that she is still here, and it would mean that you were tangled up in lies. Silence is easier for you, and it cannot hurt Monica, who has gone beyond any power of ours to hurt her.'

'I suppose you are right,' Marcia agreed.

'I know I am right.'

'Dear Janet, you always loved me best. I suppose that was hard on Monica.'

'Not a bit of it. Monica did not care a straw about me. She had a narrow heart and you were the only one she could take into it. Marcia, I want you to promise me something . . . it is the one thing I shall ever ask of you. I know you are fond of me, and if this was my last request you wouldn't hesitate to promise me, would you?'

Marcia turned round to Janet to look at her with wide and frightened eyes. 'But it isn't the last thing you will ask me. Don't talk like that, Janet. You scare me.'

'I don't want to scare you. No doubt I shall live to plague the life out of you with things I want you to do. But promise me all the same. Let us say it is the first big thing I have ever asked you to do for me . . . does that sound better?'

'Yes, much better, and I know what it is. I *will* promise then, even though it seems cruel to her. I won't tell anyone about her—nobody shall know I had a twin sister. Does that satisfy you, Janet?'

With a sigh of relief Janet kissed her. 'It does. You were always a girl to keep your word. Now I shall feel happier about you.'

Marcia clung to her. 'Oh Janet, come back to me. I shall miss you so. I can't live without you.'

'Now that's a wrong thing to say. You have your husband. You can live without anyone else if you have him. But don't be afraid for me, my darling. I'm not frightened for myself, be sure of that.'

'I can't think why you don't want me to be with you,' Marcia sighed. 'I could go up to London with you . . .'

'I know, but it will be easier for me to go alone. Come, Marcia, you always used to say that I knew best.'

Marcia sighed and made a murmur of assent, and Janet was satisfied. She drew Marcia close to her and kissed her, and there was nothing in her manner to suggest that in her heart she believed that she was parting from her for ever.

When Louis came into the room only a few minutes after Janet had left it, Marcia was in bed. Her long hair was plaited and tied with ribbons, her thin, lace-trimmed nightgown left her white shoulders bare. She was so beautiful in Louis's eyes that he experienced the familiar sensation of breathlessness.

She was too lovely to touch and yet he did touch her. He sat down on the side of the bed and took her hand. He thought it was as fragile and cool as a lily.

'Well, darling—do you like my mother? Can you be happy here for a time, until we find a home of our own?' he said.

If she was beautiful in his eyes, he was wonderfully handsome in hers. She loved his height and his breadth, his strength and his gentleness. She looked down at his brown hand which had covered hers, then up into his face. She gazed as though she would imprint every detail on her memory; the rugged features, the firm mouth which for her could soften to such an extreme tenderness, the smiling eyes which were so eloquent in their ardour. He loved his mother, he had many friends, she knew, but yet in this special way, which was so much greater than any other way, he was wholly hers.

She said, 'I can love your mother, if she will let me.'

'Indeed she will let you. She is very taken with you. I have told her a little about you, but you will tell her more. She is an easy person to talk to.'

Marcia's eyes were downcast as she said, 'I have so little to tell. Sometimes I think my life is like a book, with no writing at all on the first pages.'

He drew her nearer to him, so that she rested in his arms.

'That's a sweet thing for any new husband to hear. All the rest of the pages will be filled with close writing, and there are many, many pages before we shall have to write The End.'

'Oh, Louis, my darling, I hope so. I want it to be a long and happy book.'

'It will be.'

'And yet—' she sighed—'it has started with sadness. I am unhappy about Janet—afraid for her . . .'

'She will be all right, my sweet. In a little while she will be with us again.'

He shut his mind upon the falseness of his words. He did not believe in them, but he told himself that it was necessary to comfort Marcia, most necessary that her first few days at least, here in his home, should be unclouded. Her sweet face was pale and her eyes shadowed. It had been an ordeal for her to meet his mother. She had been dreading it, he knew, ever since they set foot in England. But now it was over, and he had faith in Alma. Marcia was his sweet and human love, but she was also, as he had said, his faerie wife. It was comforting to realize that in Alma there was also an evasive other-worldliness which would help her to understand Marcia.

3

At intervals during the next day, Toni's thoughts were fixed on Meadow House and its occupants. She had plenty to do and she did her best to detach her mind from Louis and his bride, but it was beyond her power.

Stella, her stepmother, had a headache that morning, and chose to lie in bed. It could not have been a particularly severe headache, for she enjoyed her breakfast on a tray, and now through the long sunny hours she lay there, looking quite beautiful and excessively discontented, turning over letters which had come for her by the morning post, and occasionally dipping her hand into a box of chocolates.

But although Toni did not believe in the headache, she was quite willing to have Stella out of the way. Too often she would fill the house with her lamentations. In her opinion life had been relentlessly hard on her. She had married, as she thought, to have a good time. Her husband had promised her that. They were to travel, to live in luxury, to spend much of their time in London—to have a flat there. And when they had been married only a short time, her husband fell hopelessly ill, and could not be moved.

Medical expenses were heavy and the one piece of good fortune was that Toni, who did not require a salary, returned to nurse her father. Stella was now most friendly to Toni—that was the easiest way. They understood one another. Toni loved her father and only asked to be allowed to look after him without interference. Stella would not interfere if Toni would take the management of the house as well as the nursing of Everard Benham upon her shoulders.

What she required from Toni was an uncritical attitude. It wasn't any good for her to stay at home and mope, Stella argued, and it was also useless to give more than a few minutes of her time to her husband. Poor soul, she thought, he wasn't really a man any longer, only one who was half-dead and waiting to be wholly dead, which surely must be within a short while. Then she would be free, and such money as there was would be hers. Until then she was forced to endure the situation, but as was natural, she contrived to have as good a time as it was possible to have in a country place. She had friends in the nearby town, and she was still young and good-looking, and men admired her.

The slight headache this morning was the result of a late party the night before. She felt languid and despondent and for once she was willing for Toni to take the landau for shopping which she generally monopolized. Stella asked her to buy some of the newest magazines and to call at the dressmaker's for a blouse which should be ready.

This Toni promised to do, but first she made her father comfortable for the day, gave him his breakfast and settled him in his wheelchair in a shady spot in the garden. She consulted the cook about the lunch, and told her that she would have a meal in the town. Then at last she was free to drive off, having told Stella that it would be impossible for her to get back until the late afternoon.

Stella grumbled at this, but not too much. She had invited a couple of friends to tea. They could have it out in the garden. Annie, the housemaid, would have taken Everard in for his afternoon sleep by then. She was a strong and kindly girl, and devoted to the sick man, for she had been in his service before his marriage to Stella. Toni sometimes thought it would have been impossible for her to manage without Annie.

She decided that on her homeward way she would call at Meadow House. Better get it over, she thought. She had to meet Louis some time, and the longer that meeting was delayed the more difficult it would be to carry it off naturally. The only sensible thing to do was to behave as she would have normally done, had Louis returned without a bride, and without saying those last words to her. Certainly in the days when their friendship had been no more than friendship, and therefore free from self-consciousness, she would have taken the first opportunity to see him. She would have been eager to hear all he had done while he had been away. Alma had always welcomed her, had taken it for granted that she would come and go as she chose. Even if she had not liked Toni she would have welcomed her, because Louis was always so pleased to see her. Louis had certainly been spoiled all his life by his parents, his friends, and now by his public who applauded him.

Slowly at last, her shopping accomplished, and Stella's messages fulfilled, Toni drove the landau up the drive to Meadow House. There was nobody in the garden, but through the open windows of the drawing-room voices came to her. She stood there on the threshold, dazzled with the sunshine and gazing into the room.

A slender, tall girl was arranging carnations in a vase, and that alone was rather extraordinary, for Alma prized her carnations, and rarely plucked them. But now she sat in a big chair, smiling, because the girl's hands were inexpert. The carnations looped forlornly over the rim of the vase, and collapsed upon one another.

Toni came in through the open window and said, 'That vase is not tall enough, and it's too wide at the base. There's the smaller pale green crystal one, in which slim, bare-stalked flowers look well.'

While Marcia stared, Alma rose and went to Toni and kissed her. She was grateful because she had made this unceremonious entrance and had spoken spontaneously.

Taking Toni by the hand she led her towards Marcia.

'This,' she said, 'is Toni Benham. You remember we were talking about her last night. Toni, this is Marcia, Louis's wife.'

Toni said frankly, as she held out her hand, 'Of course I knew it must be. I've been eager to meet you. It was so exciting when we heard of the wedding. I do hope we shall be friends.'

'Oh yes, I hope so too. I was telling Alma I had never had a girl friend, and I was interested when I heard you were about my own age, and that you lived near.'

'Surely I must be a lot older than you,' Toni said, surveying Marcia with interest and open admiration.

Louis's wife was certainly very beautiful and very youthful. The pale skin and the long falling hair contributed to this illusion of childishness; so did her slender figure, the wide innocence of her eyes and her voice, which was sweet and rather high, lacking the tones of maturity.

Toni's heart sank very low. It would not, she knew, have benefited her in any way had Marcia been commonplace and unlovable, for marriage was marriage, in Toni's eyes; a sacrament which nothing but death could annul, and yet it would have been less hurtful to have met an ordinary being, instead of this extraordinarily lovely creature, whom any man would find it easy to worship. It is never easy to realize that one has been outclassed, which was a thing Toni did now realize.

'I'm twenty-two,' Marcia said.

Toni glanced at Alma. 'It's hard to believe, isn't it?' she said.

Alma's gaze at Toni was an accolade. Courage was something to admire supremely, and Toni was certainly showing courage. By her casual manner, nobody could have supposed that Louis meant anything in particular to her.

'Yes,' she agreed. 'I thought when I saw Marcia last night that she was probably no more than seventeen. But then, as she has told me, until the last few months she led a very quiet, sheltered life.'

'Too sheltered,' Marcia said. 'Nobody should be. I've

thought as much over and over again since I've seen something of the world. I was telling Alma that I want to give a little shelter to people who have never had any. Louis said you were a nurse, so I thought you might be able to help me.'

'How? I don't understand,' Toni said.

'Well, don't you know lots of sick people, or couldn't you put me in touch with some?'

Intrigued and amused, in spite of the dull pain at her heart, which had not ceased to press upon it for the last twenty-four hours, Toni shook her head.

'I've not been nursing in England for the last four years,' she said. 'I'm quite out of touch with hospital life, and even if I were not, I don't see how I could help you, or even what kind of help you want.'

'I have a lot of money,' Marcia said. 'Far too much for just Louis and me. I'd like to start something, a home, which would take sick people and look after them and make them happy. Louis is willing, but he says he wants it to be something personal, which will be interesting for me, because I shall see just how much my money will do, and I could get to know people and perhaps make friends with them.'

'What an extraordinary girl you must be,' Toni exclaimed in astonishment.

'I don't see why.'

'Well, most girls couldn't have too much money. They would spend it easily enough on a beautiful home, and on jewels and furs and clothes.'

'I like all those things, but not too many of them, and there will be enough money left to make a home for us, which will be as beautiful as we can possibly imagine. Though I'm not in a hurry about that. It's lovely to be here, in the house where Louis has always lived, and it's loveliest of all to know Alma is pleased to have me.'

She threw Alma a tender glance, and Toni thought that it would have been impossible not to like this beautiful and ingenuous creature. Ingenuous and yet she sensed something unusual about her that might almost be called mysterious.

'I want to buy a big house and turn it into a convalescent home. Surely it shouldn't be difficult,' Marcia said.

'I suppose,' answered Toni slowly, 'that nothing is insurmountably difficult, if one is sufficiently determined.'

'I am determined. I've been thinking about it so much, wishing for it so much, ever since I was free.'

'Free?' echoed Toni, and it crossed her mind to wonder if Marcia had been married before, and if so whether she had been widowed or divorced.

Alma said, 'Marcia means since her mother died and she inherited all this money.'

On the words, Louis came in. Automatically Toni braced herself. Without knowing that she was doing so, she called to her aid all the pride of her female ancestors, all the duplicity which women throughout the ages have used as a protective shield.

The smile she turned upon him seemed to herself to be stiff and forced, but to Louis it appeared entirely natural, as was her voice when she said, 'Louis, how wonderfully well you look. I came over to meet your wife and to congratulate you.'

He was less clever than she at concealing his feelings. His eyes flickered as they met hers, and his voice was constrained as he said, 'That's very sweet of you, Toni. Thank you. Marcia was eager to meet you.'

Marcia went to him and linked her arm in his, and Toni watched her without wincing, as she leant against him, smiling up into his face.

'I've been telling Toni about my plan to make a home for sick people. I hoped she could help me, but she says she can't. I believe she thinks I'm too young to be serious.'

'Indeed I don't,' Toni protested. 'On the contrary, I think it is when we are young that we *are* most serious, because we are full of hope for the world. But actually I don't know how to help you, at least I haven't had time to think whether I can in any way . . . although now it does occur to me . . .'

'Yes, go on,' Marcia said eagerly, as she stopped.

Toni looked at Louis. 'Do you want me to help her?' she asked.

'Certainly, if you can, but I've told Marcia she will have to go slowly. She will defeat her own ends if she rushes things.'

'Then what I meant to tell you was that since you have been away, The Red Towers at Seacrest has been advertised for sale. There was an auction, but the house was withdrawn from sale because the reserve was not reached. Now it will be sold privately, I suppose.'

'That great tomb of a place,' Louis said.

'My dear,' Alma put in, 'you will require a big house if you intend to start a home for a dozen patients or more. I dare say you would have to spend quite a large amount on bringing The Red Towers up to date, but it's in a good position, looking out on the sea, and although I've never been in it, I hear there are many small rooms, which for an ordinary private house might be a disadvantage, but not for a home where you would probably want the bedrooms to be of little more than cubicle size.'

'Oh Louis, could we look over it?' Marcia asked.

'Of course. Naturally, to find the house would be the first thing. Afterwards I suppose the proper procedure would be to get in touch with a hospital or some doctor with a poor practice who would be interested.'

'I know such a doctor,' Toni said. 'I met him when I was training in London. He was only a medical student then, but he was intending to work with his father, who had an East End practice. He was a very idealistic person . . . very spiritual . . . a Catholic. I liked him, though he breathed a more rarefied air than I could breathe. He wrote to me once or twice while I was in America. We were friends in a sort of way.'

'He sounds the type,' Louis said thoughtfully.

Marcia squeezed his arm. 'Oh Louis, we are making real progress,' she said.

'Would you care for me to write to Richard Carlyn?' Toni asked.

To her astonishment she was so interested that she was taken right out of herself, removed from the narrow orbit of pain in which she had been blindly circulating.

'Why yes, that wouldn't be a bad idea,' Louis agreed.

'Tell him that we have not gone one step as yet towards any concrete plan, but you can tell him too that my wife is an enthusiast who is not likely to let any minor difficulties stand in her way.'

'I'll do that,' Toni promised. 'I might ask Richard to come down to stay for a long week-end in the early autumn. Father met him once and liked him, and I think it would be a tonic to him to have a talk with Richard, who always keeps cheerful, though I can't imagine how he can, for he's surrounded by unspeakable misery in his East End practice.'

'It would be wonderful to meet him,' Marcia said. 'He seems just the kind of person I want to meet.' And then she added sincerely and ingenuously, 'Isn't Louis good to let me do this?'

Louis laughed and said, 'Well, after all, my sweet, it *is* your own money.'

'That doesn't make any difference. My mother told me once that it was because she wanted to spend her money according to her own tastes that she and my father couldn't get on. He loathed the country and a quiet life and she loved it.'

'And which do you prefer, Marcia?' Alma asked.

'Something of both, I think. London and Paris and all the big cities are interesting, because of the theatres and the museums and picture galleries and all the history which is wrapped up in them, but the country is beautiful. It's much more gentle and there are all the flowers and the changing seasons. You wouldn't notice them much in a town.'

'The country to live in, and the towns to visit. That's a very good choice,' Alma said.

Alma walked round the garden with her arm linked in Toni's. It had not been difficult to detach her from the others, who, as was only natural, showed every disposition to be alone at this early stage of their marriage.

'You were wonderful, Toni,' Alma said, and realized as she spoke that she had betrayed her knowledge of Toni's love for Louis.

But Toni did not seem to mind. Her expression was thoughtful, and she said, 'I suppose you guessed that before he went away Louis thought he cared enough for me to ask me to marry him. He didn't actually, but he made his state of mind pretty clear to me.'

Alma said with relief, 'I'm so glad you felt you could tell me. You're so dear to me, so near to me, and that has made it difficult to pretend I didn't know. Louis has behaved badly to you. He's spoilt, too used to getting everything he wants.'

'I don't consider he behaved badly. I hadn't told him I loved him. Probably he has persuaded himself by now that I don't, and I shall do my best by my manner to convince him he is right. Then it will be easier for all of us. Don't look sad, Alma, I shall get over it. I expect I shall always be very fond of him, but it's possible to sublimate any emotion.'

'You're too young to have to sublimate love,' Alma said. 'I only hope you will meet someone else, who will see what a wonderful person you are.'

Toni smiled. 'Well, perhaps I shall one day. Meanwhile, as Louis has married, I am thankful it is Marcia. She's the sweetest girl, isn't she?'

'Yes, she's sweet, but . . .'

'Oh Alma, surely there's no "but" in it—not with that girl.'

'She's captivated you, I see, and so she has me, but yet there's something mysterious about her . . .'

'I feel that too, but isn't it accounted for by the strange life she has led? I gathered quite a bit through the general conversation. Her mother must have been an embittered, disappointed woman and she made the child pay for it. It's a crying scandal that she should have had to live such a life. Even her education must have been rudimentary judged by modern standards.'

'Yes, though Miss Cameron is an intelligent woman, and she told me she was a good musician and needlewoman, besides being very well read. Louis says Marcia has a gift for drawing and painting, though she has never had any tuition. She can catch a likeness and has a great sense of colour. He thinks she ought to attend art classes, and when I told Marcia that the top room could be turned into a sort of studio for her, she was delighted. I would like them to stay with me for a year or more, if that suits them.'

'It seems as though it might, especially if Marcia sinks all her energies in starting this Home she is so keen about. It's rather marvellous that anyone so young should care about those who are unfortunate.'

'Yes, but that again is partly due to her upbringing. We, who have led ordinary lives, are conditioned to suffering which I agree is terrible. We harden ourselves to it. But the knowledge of dire and degrading poverty came upon Marcia as a revelation, and she immediately saw the way in which she could put her money—of which she has far more than she needs—to a good use.'

'I do hope you will come to love her. I'm sure she needs love—not only Louis's, but a woman's.'

Alma squeezed Toni's arm. 'Really, you're the dearest girl. Nobody else in your position would care twopence whether or not she was happy. But I agree that she's lovable, though as I say there's something . . .'

'What?'

'I feel she's hiding something,' Alma said. 'Something terribly important and vital, which might even have prevented Louis from marrying her. I haven't the least idea what it is, and I've nothing to go on, only that much overworked intuitive gift which women are supposed to possess.'

'You do possess it,' Toni said. 'But in this case don't you think it may be just prejudice, because Louis married an unknown girl, and because you love me and hoped he would marry me?'

'No—I don't think it's prejudice. Actually Marcia quite fascinated me from the moment I met her, but you know how it was with me before I even knew of their marriage—I had the most horrible presentiment of disaster. Since then I've been constantly beating it down, which isn't so difficult when I am actually with her.'

'But,' said Toni, distressed and genuinely puzzled, 'how can you think there is any fear of disaster? Obviously Marcia is good and beautiful and intelligent . . . she's so innocent that it's almost piteous.'

'I know all that . . . but all the same I wish Louis had never met her. I can love her and I shall, but I shall still wish it.'

'But Alma, it all seems so irrational.'

'It is.' Alma sighed. 'Toni . . . I want to tell you a strange thing which happened. I don't know if you will believe me. Probably you will think me mad . . . I'd almost rather I was mad. Louis and Marcia arrived yesterday, I went out to meet them, and as Louis greeted me, I naturally looked beyond him to see his wife and form my first impression of her . . . and Toni, there were three people sitting in the carriage . . .'

'Three! But how could there be? There were only Marcia and Miss Cameron who has gone into hospital.'

'Nevertheless there *were* three people. A dark girl was just behind Marcia—very close to her, it was as though she leant against her. She was young, and I realize now there was a resemblance, though Marcia is fair, and this girl was dark; dark-haired, dark-skinned, and dark with evil. I stared at her and she stared back at me, and I swear there was amusement in her eyes and a kind of triumph. She was defying me, for it was as though wave upon wave of wickedness was wafted from her to me. I put my hands up to my face because I could not endure it, and then when at last I looked again, she wasn't there . . . only Marcia and Miss Cameron and Louis beside me. The dark girl had gone. I had seen an evil vision . . . and I fainted.'

Toni was silent. It was impossible not to be impressed, but it was equally impossible to believe. She said at last, 'You must have imagined it.'

'That's the obvious explanation. I wish I could accept it.'

'But if it were true—if you really did have a supernatural experience, what is the meaning of it? Surely you don't think that evil face was a projection of Marcia's personality?'

'Oh, good heavens, no!' cried Alma with genuine horror.

'Then there doesn't seem to be any sense in it,' Toni said.

'I see no meaning in it myself, but I know there is one. Oh, Toni, Louis is so dear to me. I can't bear to think that he will be hurt, that his life will be ruined.'

'How can you think that that child could ruin his life? Why he's a god to her, you can see it when she looks at him. She will do whatever he wishes, always.'

'Probably I'm being ridiculous,' Alma said. 'But I wanted you to know about that—experience. Some day we may understand it.'

Toni, as she drove back to her own home, had sufficient to think about. She had faith in Alma's psychic gift, and could not believe that she had imagined the thing which she had told her.

She was conscious of fear, of apprehension, and was unable to shake off this sensation. It was strange, she thought, that her personal pain should have receded, for now it did not seem to matter much to her that she had had such a cruel disappointment. Her thoughts dwelt worriedly on Louis and on Marcia. Being reasonable as well as unselfish, she wanted them to be happy, for what good would it do her if they were not?

But when she entered the house, she forgot for the time being to think of either of them, for Stella was out and her father had been seized by one of his periodical attacks of deep depression.

In the effort to dispel this, Toni forgot the uncanny fear which Alma had implanted. She was even glad that she had interesting news for her father, since she had not as yet told him that Louis was married.

She did so now, describing this beautiful and unusual bride in detail; telling him too of her plan to use some portion of her money to start a Home for the poor and the sick.

Everard Benham was keenly interested, and begged Toni to bring Marcia over to see him as soon as possible. Fortunately he had not the slightest suspicion that Louis was more to Toni than any old friend. He had not had any chance to see them together of late. Stella also, as Toni knew, would be equally obtuse. She was too wrapped up in herself to be observant.

A lonely sorrow was easier to bear than one which was known and discussed by one's family, but Alma's knowledge of the state of affairs was bearable. In fact Toni welcomed it, because she knew that the secret they shared brought Alma even nearer to her.

When she was alone that evening she sat down at her writing desk and wrote to Richard Carlyn. His last letter received by her some months ago was still unanswered, and after apologizing for her long silence, she went on to tell him of Louis's marriage, and the wish of his wife to benefit people who were in need of a holiday or special attention. There was a possible house in the neighbourhood, and Toni had a hunch that they would snap it up. If they did, would Richard be interested in the plan? He might be able to send the right type of invalids to the Home. Anyway it would be a great pleasure to her and to her father if he could take the time off and come down to Devon for a week or so. Then he could meet Louis and his wife and discuss the plan with them.

She brought the letter to an end, signed her name, put the sheet of notepaper into an envelope and addressed and stamped it, ready for the post tomorrow.

She was fairly certain that her invitation would be accepted. Only his own illness or a terrific pressure of work would induce Richard to refuse it. Realizing this, she frowned slightly, Richard had been in love with her for years, but she was not in the least in love with him. Nevertheless she liked and admired him, and now it seemed to her that she might do worse than to marry him.

She could not leave her father, but she knew sadly enough that his days were drawing to a close. His heart was fatally weak and his general state of health was much worse than it had been six weeks ago. He might live for another year, though the doctor had told her it was improbable, but in any case Richard would wait for her.

As his wife, with her nursing experience she could be of great help to him, and the life would interest her and stimulate her. She was not afraid of hardship or of ugly sights. The burning desire of her heart, now that Louis was lost to her, was to be of use to the world, and of paramount importance to some other human being.

She sighed. Put into words it all sounded very reasonable and very barren. For it was in her nature to want to give love, not merely to accept it.

4

Two days later news was received of Janet's death. Louis, who knew that the operation had been scheduled to take place that morning, telephoned the hospital late in the afternoon, to be told that Miss Cameron had died under the anaesthetic.

Louis turned from the telephone with a sense of dread which almost obscured his pity and regret. He was thankful that Marcia had not been there to listen to the conversation and gather what had happened, before he could find a way of preparing her for the shock. But Alma, passing across the hall as he replaced the receiver, saw his worried face.

'Have you had news from the hospital?' she asked.

'Yes. She's gone.'

'Oh, dear, I was afraid . . .' Pity and distress moulded Alma's features. 'I'm sure she didn't expect to recover, but Marcia had no idea. It will be terrible for her—that nice woman. She was so brave and so sane, and she was devoted to Marcia.'

Louis said, 'She guessed it was hopeless, that's why she was so anxious to hurry on our marriage. It wouldn't have mattered so much to Janet, had she been sure that she would be out and about again in a few weeks.'

'Who will break it to Marcia? Where is she?' Alma asked.

'She's with Toni, visiting her father. He wanted to meet

her. She'll be back after tea.'

Saying that he personally could do with something stronger than tea, Louis went into the dining-room, and poured himself a stiff whisky and soda. He carried it into the drawing-room where Alma was sitting. Hetty brought in tea, and Alma poured out for herself, while Louis drank his whisky.

'Poor little thing,' Alma said. 'She has so few friends, and Janet was more like a mother to her. She's bound to take it hardly.'

'Yes, but Marcia has courage, and it will be some comfort to her to know that Janet didn't suffer. But, oh God, I wish the poor child had had a different sort of life. The sooner I can see her surrounded by a host of friends, the better.'

'That's unselfish of you,' said Alma. 'Most men with such a beautiful wife would want to keep her wholly to themselves.'

He shook his head. 'Love doesn't take me that way. I'm not particularly possessive, and I shun the responsibility of being the one and only person in anyone's life. I want to be first, certainly, but I should hate to think that if I died Marcia would be as solitary as she was when I first met her. When she has got over the first shock and grief of this, I want to give a party. We could ask four or five people and put them up for the week-end, couldn't we?'

'Certainly. There are three spare rooms, and a bed could be put in the room we are turning into a studio for Marcia. It would be a very good idea. Who do you plan to ask?'

'I hadn't really got round to thinking of that, but I might ask some writing people down from London. There's Cosmo Gallion, the book critic on the *Meteor*, he's been a very good friend to me, and James Panfrey, my agent, and his wife, and Virginia Challis, and her son.'

'The actress?' asked Alma with lively interest. 'Has she a son? A grown-up one?'

'Yes—Denis must be twenty-seven or eight.'

'Good gracious! I wouldn't have thought she was old enough.'

'Virginia is fifty if she is a day,' said Louis, amused.

'I can't think how women manage it. She still looks almost a girl. Well, it would certainly be very exciting to have her here as a guest, if you think she wouldn't find it all too simple for her.'

'Virginia's a simple person. She likes nothing better when she is not working than to lounge about in shabby clothes and slippers. I am sure . . .' he broke off as they both heard footsteps crunching the gravel, and the sound of voices.

'That's Marcia now, and Toni has come back with her,' Alma said.

In silence they both looked towards the open windows, through which the two girls a few minutes later entered the room. Marcia was flushed and animated. She had enjoyed her conversation with Everard Benham, who had been in one of his best moods and had shown the keenest interest in her idealistic plans. But as she looked from Louis to Alma, the light died out of her eyes, and she said, 'Did you telephone the hospital?'

Louis bent his head in assent. He went to Marcia and took her hands. 'My dear, I'm so grieved for you. She died under the anaesthetic,' he said.

Marcia looked at him with blank eyes. 'Oh no, oh no, that can't be,' she cried. 'Janet wouldn't . . . she knows I couldn't bear it . . .'

'My poor darling.' Louis put his arms around her and held her close. 'She knew you would have me, and that I should love you and care for you.'

'But you don't understand,' Marcia cried wildly. 'She was the only one, the only one who knew . . .'

'Knew what?' Alma asked, and although her voice was gentle, it was also insistent.

Marcia swung round to face her. She tore her hands from Louis's grasp, and they flew to cover her mouth. It was as though she literally pressed back betraying words.

'Nothing . . . I don't know . . . nothing!' she gasped.

Her lovely face was suddenly convulsed with grief, with terror, with desolation. She stood for an instant staring at them, and then it was as though the strength went out of her, for she sank down on the floor moaning softly. It was then that Toni came forward. She knelt beside Marcia and partially raised her. The girl's eyes were open, but they were glassy, a fleck of foam showed at the edge of her lips. She was not unconscious and yet it was obvious that she was far beyond the reach of their soothing words.

'It—it—is it a fit?' Alma whispered, and the thought passed through her mind that this might be the mystery. Marcia might be an epileptic, and the fact had been concealed from Louis.

Toni stood up as Louis lifted his wife in his arms, and, suspecting Alma's thought, she said, 'No—not really, but she has had a great shock, and needs to be treated for shock.'

'I should have broken it to her more carefully,' Louis said with remorse.

'You couldn't. There *is* no way of breaking a crushing tragedy. No, don't lay her down on the sofa. It would be better to carry her upstairs, then I can get her to bed. Could you see about some hot water bottles—she's cold, and some strong sweet coffee would be helpful. No—' in answer to Louis's interrogation—'I don't think it's necessary to telephone the doctor. I can cope . . . if you will let me. The first thing is to get her to bed.'

Without knowing why, Toni wanted to be alone with Marcia, and luckily, probably because she was a nurse, Louis made no objection to leaving them together, when he had carried Marcia upstairs to her bedroom.

'I'll call you, when I've brought her properly round,' Toni said. 'Hurry up those hot water bottles and the coffee,' and then she smiled reassuringly at him, and said, 'Don't be scared. It's not serious.'

When Louis had left, she started to get Marcia undressed, and into bed. Marcia was not unconscious, but she was limp and seemed incapable of helping herself. Her eyes were fixed in a piteous expression of fear, and as Toni pulled the eiderdown over her, she started to talk in a rambling, disjointed manner.

'She's dead, and I know you don't care . . . you're glad. She stood between us . . . she helped me, but now she's not here, and you will have more power. Oh, why can't you leave me alone? Why can't you? Why can't you?'

Toni sat down on the bed and took Marcia's hands firmly within her own. This was hysteria, a common enough phenomenon to her, and one with which she was thoroughly competent to deal. 'Marcia, pull yourself together. I'm with you. There's nothing to be afraid of . . . there's nobody here but you and I.'

But the words uttered with confidence rang strangely in the room, and suddenly Toni herself was conscious of fear. A shiver glided down her spine, and it was as though a derisive laugh echoed in her ears. But it wasn't a laugh which anyone else would have heard; it was something which she knew and heard with her mind. Knowing this she nevertheless glanced round the room, seeking reassurance. As she did so, she realized that Marcia's eyes, completely normal now, observed her, and suddenly the girl clutched at her sleeve.

'Toni, be my friend. Now Janet has gone I have nobody,' she cried piteously.

'My dear, that's not true.' Toni bent down to her compassionately. 'I know she was your oldest friend, but you have Louis and Alma, and of course you have me. Certainly I will be your friend.'

'You're strong,' said Marcia. 'You might even be stronger than she.'

'What do you mean, Marcia?'

The girl sighed and closed her eyes. 'She's gone now,' she said.

It was true, Toni thought. Whatever alien spirit had been with them in the room had departed. It was fantastic, but she could not feel that it was fantastic. An instant ago her very spirit had crept, not so much with terror, as with loathing.

'Marcia, can't you tell me what you mean, tell me what is troubling you?' she coaxed.

Marcia shook her head. 'I daren't—not now—but perhaps some day. Only please help me, Toni, please pray for me. There *is* such a prayer, isn't there? Doesn't one ask to be delivered from the darkness and dangers of the night?

That needn't only mean an ordinary night, but the night of —of the soul.'

Toni felt the tears start to her eyes for there was such fear and pleading in the girl's voice. 'But of course I will— one does pray I suppose even when one is not particularly religious, and I will pray that you shan't be made afraid, that you may be happy, and that you will bless Louis with your love.'

'Oh, poor Louis,' Marcia sighed.

'Lucky Louis because he has you.'

Marcia sighed sadly. 'Perhaps he shouldn't have married me, but Janet said it would be right. She said I could give him as much as I took from him, that there was no reason why I shouldn't make him happy. I went to church and prayed about it, and I thought I had an answer.'

'I expect you did.'

'I do want to be good and do good,' Marcia said pathetically. 'Are you sure that one's prayers get answered?'

'Well, I was told so as a child, and Richard Carlyn would assure you that they do.'

'Richard Carlyn?'

'The doctor I told you about, to whom I've written about your wish to start a convalescent home. He is a Catholic and he has a deep sense of religion.'

'It must be lovely for anyone who has. I was never taught anything—not really. My mother was quite uninterested. Janet was a Calvinist, but her religion seemed so grim and unyielding. When I went with her into her church it didn't say anything to me, but the beautiful old churches on the Continent did.'

'I dare say we all confuse beauty with holiness,' Toni mused.

Marcia was sitting up in bed now and her eyes were clear. 'It must mean something to want to be good, and that truly is my greatest wish. Toni, I'm terribly keen to buy this house. I want Louis to come with me tomorrow to look at it, and I hope he won't find too many objections. I could make it a memorial to Janet, couldn't I?'

'Certainly you could.'

'Louis is rather cautious though, as I suppose most men

are. They think and plan, while women leap ahead, sometimes to their mortification.'

'But sometimes to a success,' said Toni, 'which men lose because they haven't the courage to leap.'

Louis did find plenty of faults with The Red Towers when he and Marcia eventually applied to the agents for an order to view, and went over it together. But he also admitted some outstanding advantages.

The house was, as they agreed, set in an ideal position for a convalescent home. It was built on a small promontory overlooking the sea, and at the back of the house there was a rambling, untended garden. There was an orchard and also space for a croquet lawn; a nice, leisurely game for people who were not very strong, said Marcia.

From the structural angle the house was ugly in the extreme. It was built of red brick and its oldest wing dated back from early Victorian days. Successive owners had added to it with more lavishness than taste, and the two towers which topped it contained practically useless small rooms, reached by a narrow iron staircase which twisted perilously.

Only a tight-rope walker, Louis said scathingly, would find it easy to get up and down to the towers, from the main part of the sprawling house.

Marcia stood by his side looking out of one of the narrow windows. 'Perhaps they were built for the view,' she said. 'That's wonderful enough. On a clear day one would be able to see for miles around.'

Louis conceded the view but doubted if it was worth the difficult climb to see it. It would be just as easy to walk to the top of a hill, and then you would also get the benefit of the fresh air. His acrimonious mood failed him, however, when he glanced at Marcia's downcast face. The poor child, he thought remorsefully, she had set her heart on this and it was cruel of him to damp her pleasure. But it did occur to him as strange that while she could make absorbing plans for a philanthropic object, she appeared to have so little interest in plans for themselves. Certainly these were early days, but when he had spoken of looking out for a house of their own, she had said something vague about being happy with Alma, about loving her little studio, and then with more decision she had pointed out that she knew nothing whatever about housekeeping, and wanted time to learn.

His faerie wife! It was an apt description, for she was so often away in a world of her own. She did not deliberately bar him out, but he felt an intruder there. She loved him, but for hours at a time she could contentedly read or work in her studio. She was happy in his company, but he sometimes had the feeling that she would be equally happy without it.

For a time after Janet's death, Marcia had been in low spirits, but after a while it was as though Janet faded from her mind, for she rarely spoke of her.

Louis had started a new book and was slightly compunctious because his work entailed privacy and silence. He had urged Marcia to be with Toni as much as she could, saying that it worried him to think of her loneliness. There was Alma, of course, but she after all was of a different generation.

'But I'm never alone,' Marcia said, and then, guiltily, the colour had swept over her face and the furtive expression to which he was becoming accustomed clouded her eyes.

He had dismissed this remark, taking it that she meant she had her books and her sketching block and various other employments for company. But oddly, the memory of that burning blush, that evident embarrassment came back to him later on.

He could not explain it, and it seemed to be quite unimportant, but nevertheless he was beginning to realize that there were many trivial things about Marcia which puzzled him. Even as a lover she had oddly opposing moods. Sometimes she was all his, at others not his at all.

Because these thoughts were discomforting he tried to dismiss them, and he did so now, putting his arm round her as they stood together at the window, pleased to see her so wholly absorbed and satisfied. It was because of this pleasure that he surrendered without more ado.

'Very well, my sweet, buy the place if you really want it. The price is not too stiff. It will need reconstructing though, and if you take my advice you'll get in touch with a first-class architect.'

'Darling Louis, of course I shall take your advice,' Marcia said. 'Oh, I'm so happy about it. I love the house and it will be wonderful when there are more windows, all looking out on the sea or the garden; and of course we want at least three more bathrooms. As Alma said, the small bedrooms are an advantage, for then everyone can have a separate one. I want to make them all individual. Every room can be a different colour, or blend of colours, and have a different type of picture on the walls, and they must all have fitted carpets to match the curtains and bedspreads.'

'You're planning for this to be a home for women, I take it,' Louis said, and for an instant Marcia looked quite comically blank. Then she said, 'I must be, though I've never consciously told myself so. It would be difficult to mix men and women, and anyway I'm not particularly interested in men. I don't understand them, and I don't feel for them as I do for women. That's not very fair of me, is it?'

'Well, I don't know; on the whole I think it's fair enough, since you happen to be a woman. Men have more done for them, and certainly you couldn't interest yourself as intensely in a home which was run for men.'

'When you are a terribly famous author, turning out a bestseller each year, which brings you in thousands and thousands of pounds, you can start a convalescent home for men,' Marcia suggested.

Louis shouted with laughter. 'Not on your life! I'd far rather buy the biggest diamonds I could find to string round your neck,' he said.

Toni, who saw much of Marcia, was charmed because she was busy and happy. Now that The Red Towers had been bought, Marcia was over there every day, and Toni, who had been convinced that there was something strange and abnormal about her, was now able to dismiss her fears until Louis, coming in search of Marcia one day, when he supposed that she was with Toni, aroused in her a fresh anxiety.

They strolled round the garden together, for Stella had taken Marcia into Seacrest to do some odds and ends of shopping.

'They won't be long,' said Toni. 'Stella is bound to be back before six, for she has arranged a small sherry party, and she will have to change before the guests arrive. By the way, she wanted you and Marcia to come.'

'Does Marcia want to?' asked Louis. 'I loathe sherry parties, and the kind of people who mainly go to them and stand propping up the walls talking to one or two friends with complete disregard for the rest of the guests.'

'Oh, I agree,' Toni said. 'Parties are rarely maty. No, I don't think Marcia's keen to stay.'

'Good for her. Though I want her to make friends, and I'm arranging a week-end house-party for next month. I hope you'll come over as often as possible. Some of these people will probably interest you.'

'I'm sure they will, but I have Richard Carlyn staying here for a fortnight about the same time. I heard from him yesterday. He's very interested in Marcia's plan for a convalescent home. He will be only too eager to help.'

'That's good,' Louis said. 'Bring him over with you when you come, we shall be delighted.' And then he added after a pause, 'I really wish he would see Marcia as a doctor. She refuses to see Price, it seems that she has a deep antipathy to medicos.'

'But isn't that a healthy sign? A well person never does like a doctor in a professional sense. Marcia seems to me to be in perfect health. She was knocked over by Miss Cameron's death, but she has recovered from it.'

'All the same I should be more at ease if she had a routine check-over. She had extensive operations after that accident in which her mother was killed. She won't speak of it to me and I feel it might be harmful to press her, but sometimes I wonder if there were head injuries . . .'

Toni burst out laughing. 'Oh, Louis, you can't think there is anything mentally wrong with Marcia. I'm with her so much that I should know. She's been absorbed, thrilled by the purchase of The Red Towers, altogether happy these last weeks.'

'Of course I'm not suggesting that, but I do often believe she is under some sort of strain. I'm conscious of a barrier; she changes so much in her moods that she might be two different girls at times.'

'That could be said of many of us.'

'Could it? Well, although I've not been married before, I doubt if most wives are as variable in their moods as Marcia. But they're scarcely a question for a doctor. What does worry me are her frequent nightmares.'

'Nightmares do suggest a nervous condition,' Toni agreed.

She was worried when she saw Louis's face. Evidently he was troubled and perplexed, more so than he intended her to guess.

'There's something on her mind,' he said. 'It happens sometimes when she is sleeping sweetly and deeply. I've felt her become rigid beside me, and then she starts to talk, not incoherently, but slowly and clearly. She talks to someone called Monica. Sometimes she begs and beseeches her to leave her alone; sometimes, last night for instance, she said, "I can't do it, Monica, I daren't do it. If I let you get right inside me there will be no me left. I'm sorry, terribly sorry, but you must stay in your place, and I must stay in mine." And then another time she sat up in bed and it was as though she pushed someone away from her, and that time she said something about belonging to me, about loving Monica, but not enough to share her very spirit with her. Last night she actually seemed to be making some sort of bargain. She said, "If I let you in for a little while, a few hours, will you promise me that I shall be able to get back again?" I know it sounds ridiculous, but it was horribly uncanny to listen to her. I couldn't stand it. I woke her up and she clung to me as though she was thankful to be back in this world again. But I couldn't persuade her to tell me about her dream—she said she remembered nothing.'

'Which was probably true,' Toni said. 'When I was in

hospital, patients would often scream and cry in a dream, so that they had to be awakened. Nine times out of ten they couldn't remember having dreamed. I wouldn't be too anxious, Louis, but I do think it will be splendid if Richard and Marcia became friendly, for then if there is anything worrying her, she may confide in him.'

'It would be a great relief to me,' Louis said simply.

Toni was shaken by compassion for him. He had been married less than three months, and yet it was plain to be seen that he was not happy, or at least not entirely happy. The talk of Marcia's nightmares revived the memory of her collapse after Janet Cameron's death. She had said wild, strange things then, talking as though a third person were in the room with them, and Toni had had the uncanny sense that they were not alone. It had been an eerie, dark experience which she had willed herself to forget, because she had not been able to explain it away.

The old forbidden longing swept through Toni's being. Oh, if only Louis had never met this strange girl, whom one could not help but love, even though one did not understand her. Toni sensed that she would be an eternal puzzle to them all: fascinating, sweet, seemingly so simple and yet with dark pockets in her soul. It was not a nature which made for happiness. Louis might love her madly, might spend hours of wild rapture with her, but he would never have the peace of trust and familiarity.

No words could express the sense of doom which struck Toni now. She could not explain it, for she could do nothing to avert it. She would have made him happy, she thought rebelliously, she could not have given him this fervour, this wild romance, but there would have been peace for his work, peace for his soul; there would have been companionship.

Her certainty that with Marcia he would find neither peace nor companionship might have been interpreted as disloyalty, but Toni was not conscious of disloyalty.

'I wish we knew more about Marcia's life before you met her,' she said slowly.

'But according to Miss Cameron there was little to know.

Marcia's mother had kept her a prisoner, remote from the world.'

'Yes—according to Miss Cameron. Oh, I don't doubt that what she told you was the truth, but was it *all* the truth? Doesn't it strike you as odd that Marcia submitted? She wasn't a child when her mother was killed, she was over twenty-one. She obeyed her implicitly, it seems—but why? She has plenty of initiative now, as witness her plans for this home. Why did Miss Cameron consent to such a life? She seems to have been a strong-minded woman. Why didn't she urge Marcia to escape? They could have gone together, and Miss Cameron would have helped her, for she must have had some money of her own. Until you look into it, it seems a simple story, but it isn't simple, not really.'

'I've told myself the same thing, a dozen times, but I have to accept Marcia's story. One thing I know: she was and is as innocent as a child.'

'Oh, I agree. I wasn't thinking of sex. It's something far more subtle—more frightening . . .'

'Toni, what in the world do you mean?'

She looked at him with dazed eyes and answered truthfully, 'I haven't the remotest idea.'

Louis shrugged impatiently: 'We're making something out of nothing. Marcia was brought up to accept an abnormal life. She knew no other existence. Perhaps until her chains were struck off, she was scarcely aware of them. As for Janet Cameron, she was no more than an employee and she was probably well paid. She adored Marcia, who was wholly hers during those years. Perhaps she thought if she helped her to her freedom she would lose her.'

'Perhaps,' Toni agreed.

She decided to keep her thoughts to herself. It would only distress Louis more if she spoke of them, though this explanation seemed to her incredible, if only because Janet Cameron had evidently been eager to give Marcia all possible freedom once her mother was dead. The mystery probably centred in Mrs Norman herself. She might have been completely out of her mind, which would account for the seclusion in which the household lived. Possibly she was dangerous and should have been in a mental home, and from this Janet Cameron and Marcia and the two faithful servants had conspired to save her.

It was a not impossible explanation, but Toni quailed at the thought that Louis might have married a girl in whom were the seeds of insanity.

'I'm thankful Richard is coming to stay,' she said. 'He's clever, and it's possible he may understand Marcia better than you or I. Anyway I know he will want to do everything he can to help her.'

5

'You look well; you've actually put on weight,' was Toni's greeting to Richard Carlyn when she met him at the railway station. And she added, 'I can't think how you manage it.'

He laughed, walking by her side down the platform.

'Why not? I'm happy and interested doing the job I love. Naturally I look well.'

'Virtue its own reward in fact.'

'I'm far from claiming virtue. All I say is that I'm happy, and most happy people have good health.'

Toni looked at him sideways. It was true he had always had this capacity for happiness, and with little reason. It was all very well to give service, but this dedicated kind of life was dreary, it seemed to her. Most people would have said that Richard was wasting his gifts in the poor district where he had his practice. So many of his patients must be beyond help because of their own hopeless natures. Tragedy, the tragedy of all poverty, was his daily portion, and he could do little to help. Surely it needed a singularly humble disposition to know that the service of your whole life would be no more than a drop in the ocean of suffering

—but then in some ways Richard was humble. Toni sighed. She admired him so much, what a pity it was that she couldn't love him. This thought had been thrust upon her when she had been walking down the platform to meet him, and had seen his face radiant with pleasure at the sight of her.

He was not a particularly good-looking young man, but there was something unforgettable about his face. His eyes were a clear grey and they were extremely expressive. He was fair and rather thick-set, only slightly above medium height. His smile was one of singular sweetness. It gave you a clue, Toni thought, to his essential goodness. He radiated loving-kindness; one felt the warmth, the humanity of his nature as a benediction.

Toni, in a rush of generous affection, was delighted to think that at last Richard was really having a holiday. Say what he might he needed a rest and a little of the comforts of life. Now for a fortnight he would be lapped in comfort. His room on the first floor was large and bright and looked out upon the garden. The weather seemed to have settled in for a warm autumn spell. It would be pleasant to see him enjoy his food, enjoy driving round the country or lazing in the sun.

But when Richard next spoke she realized that in taking a fortnight's holiday he had not been thinking solely of himself.

'I gathered from your letter that you had been pretty well tied down lately,' he said. 'It occurred to me that during this fortnight I could take some of the care of your father off your hands.'

Toni uttered an exasperated groan. 'You're too bad. Can't you think of yourself? I certainly didn't want you here for that reason. You can talk to Father, of course, cheer him up now and again, but nothing more. I want you to enjoy yourself.'

'But, my dear girl, I shall enjoy myself very much if I know I'm giving you a few hours of extra freedom,' said Richard. 'I worry about you, Toni. I was overjoyed when you returned from America because then you were within my reach, but I hate to think that your liberty is curtailed.'

'I'm willing for it to be curtailed. I only wish it would be for longer. Dr Price doesn't think that Father can live more than a few months.'

'I'm sorry, my dear.'

'I'm lucky to be here to make things better for him,' Toni said.

'Yes, indeed you are,' he agreed, and then said after a brief pause: 'Have you thought of what you will do afterwards?'

'I have—but I'm still undecided. I may as well be honest and admit that I've even turned over in my mind the possibility of marrying you. That is, if you still want me.'

'You know I shall always want you.'

'But not without love, Richard.'

'No, not without love.'

'It's out of my power to make myself care in that way. I wish it wasn't. I would like to make life more comfortable for you, to share your work. I should feel I was doing good, being of some use in the world.'

'You could never fail to be that, Toni.'

'And then there's the religious question,' she said restlessly. 'I don't belong to any church and you are a Catholic. You would expect me to become one too.'

'Yes, I should expect that,' he agreed quietly.

'But I'm not at all sure that I could. I'm in complete ignorance, or almost complete ignorance, for I do realize that to be a good Catholic you have to make endless sacrifices.'

'As though that would deter you. I know nobody who is better at making sacrifices.'

'You're so persistent,' she said discontentedly. 'Sometimes I believe you will wear me down.'

'Wear you down! Why, I scarcely see you, and I'm afraid to pester you with too many letters.'

'You're like a needle prick in my soul all the same. I'm always aware of you.'

'Toni, that's the most encouraging thing you have ever said to me. Don't look scared. I know you don't mean it to be encouraging, but it is all the same.'

'Let's talk of something else,' she said decidedly. 'I had no intention of starting a conversation such as this within a few minutes of seeing you.'

'It's quite natural. You spoke about the thing which is foremost in your mind at the moment. But now we have spoken of it we can go on to something else, your poor little rich friend for instance.'

'Why do you call her that?'

'It was the picture I got of her through your letter. She seems to have everything and nothing.'

'She should be entirely happy,' Toni said thoughtfully, 'but sometimes I think she's not conditioned to happiness, that she will have to learn to be happy just as she is now learning a new way of life. I knew you would be interested in this scheme of hers and I think you will be interested in her personally. Louis suggested that I should bring you over to Meadow House today. We could go round there after dinner.'

Richard asked if the house had actually been bought, and Toni told him it had. It would take some months for repair work, but then Marcia hoped he would be able to supply her with occupants.

There would be no difficulty about that, Richard said, once Marcia had engaged a competent staff, though no doubt there would be endless snags when the patients arrived and had to be settled in. He had found that people in the direst straits and in the direst need of assistance often fought against it. A convalescent home in the country was not the average East Londoner's idea of bliss. The isolation would appal them, and the very cleanliness of the place would affront them. So many of his patients were conditioned to living in small and crowded rooms, were conditioned to constant noise. Loneliness was their chief horror, and any suggestion of officialdom aroused their hostility.

'Marcia only wants everyone to be happy,' Toni said.

'But it's not easy to make people happy except in their own way. She will have endless disappointments I fear. However, it would be wrong to discourage her, and I certainly shan't do that.'

At Meadow House Marcia and Alma were busy making preparations for the guests who were to arrive that weekend. Marcia was thrilled about it and Alma was pleased to see her excited pleasure.

If Marcia was a puzzle to Louis, she was even more of a puzzle to Alma, who, when comparing her with other girls of her age, could only feel that this young daughter-in-law of hers was a being apart.

Marcia was never lonely, never anything but even-tempered, no trouble at all to anyone, but she remained an enigma. She behaved as though she was a guest, and an obliging one, turning up punctually for meals, making no demands on her hostess, and being always ready to fall in with any plan which was made for her. Alma often puzzled over her own discontent. For long years she had told herself that, when Louis married, she must be prepared to take second place in his life. His wife, as was natural, would come first with him, and it would need all her tact, all her good sense to preserve pleasant relations with a daughter-in-law who might at first be jealous of her.

But this problem had not been presented to her. Marcia was in love with Louis certainly, but in an odd way. She did not seem to want to be with him unless he first sought her out; she showed no possessiveness, and obviously considered that Alma had the first claim on him. Certainly she had no desire for a home of her own or to entertain for Louis. She had at first made one or two tentative efforts to learn domestic ways, but she was singularly inept and could not conceal that housekeeping bored her. She was charming when guests came to the house but did not seem particularly interested in anyone except Toni.

It was Marcia's taste for solitude which chiefly astounded Alma. She had a way of vanishing for hours on end. Louis would search for her and would find her in the most remote spot in the garden or at work in her improvised studio. She read a good deal of verse. She talked very little and this quality baffled Alma. Apart from The Red Towers and her sketching she appeared to have few interests and even the scheme for the nursing home was little discussed. The place was overrun with workmen and Marcia hated the disorder thus created, and said rather wistfully that she had lost her vision of the Home which had once been so vivid. She could not now imagine what it would be like when it was all in order, or rather she could imagine that it would be too sterilized, too orderly and standardized for anyone to find happiness there.

This in a sense Alma understood and she was too kind-hearted to voice her own feeling, which was that any convalescent home, though fulfilling an urgent need, was not the type of place in which people could be really happy. Most of those who came there would be only too eager to get away, thought Alma, who understood that a home, even if it only consisted of one dingy room, was precious because it was permanently the owner's possession and an expression of an individual personality.

It was a surprise to her that over this week-end party which Louis had arranged, Marcia showed some enthusiasm, but she discovered that this was chiefly because she wanted to meet Cosmo Gallion, the literary critic.

Some five years previously, Gallion had written a book which had made a sensation. Janet, who had been empowered to order from London any books which she thought suitable for Marcia, had ordered this one, which was set in Elizabethan days. As a rule Marcia's mother had taken very little interest in her activities, but it chanced Mrs Norman had come upon her, when she was engrossed in the book, and had lashed out in a violent rage. She had torn the book from Marcia's hands, had flung it in the fire and had heaped fresh coal upon it. The reason for this had never been made clear to Marcia; to this day it was a puzzle to her, and naturally it aroused her interest in the author.

'I've heard of the book,' Alma said, 'but I've not read it. Was there anything very startling in it?'

Marcia shook her head. 'I don't think so. It was just history, written in a fascinating sort of way.'

'There must have been something in it, though, which violently offended your mother. I don't know anything about Cosmo Gallion, except that according to Louis he is a dry, saturnine type of man. He happens to admire Louis's work and has given him some very good reviews. Then they met at some literary gathering and became friendly.'

'If he's to sleep in my studio I had better start to clear out some of my things,' Marcia said. 'I could put the easel in the box-room, and take my portfolio of sketches down to my bedroom. Louis thinks some of them are good enough to be framed, the pastels chiefly, so I must look after them.'

'I'll help you,' Alma offered.

She was aware of relief, of a sense of satisfaction, because for once Marcia seemed like the ordinary daughter-in-law that any ordinary woman might expect. She was down to earth at last, expressing a natural curiosity to meet a famous man, and actually making some constructive plan about the drawings which occupied so much of her time.

They went up the wide staircase together into the top room. Marcia picked up two bulging portfolios and Alma turned her attention to the easel upon which there was a canvas draped by a cloth. A palette and an open box of oil paints lay on the table beside it, and Alma judged by this that Marcia had turned for the time being from her crayon and black and white drawings, several of which she had seen.

Now, casually curious, Alma went to the easel and pulled back the shrouding cloth. Marcia had carried the portfolios into the box-room farther along the landing, and she came back to see Alma standing before the easel, a fold of covering cloth still in one hand, absolutely immobile, her features fixed in an expression of horror.

With a gasp Marcia sprang forward. She seized the cloth from Alma's hand and flung it over the unfinished painting. She stared at Alma silently, her face pale and twitching, her hands clenched.

'That wasn't for you to see . . . not for anyone to see,' she got out at last.

'Who is it, Marcia?' Alma asked.

'It's nobody . . . it's an imagination painting. I often do

them. I thought I would experiment with oils, and I just painted a face from my imagination. Don't look at me like that . . . it's the truth. If Janet were alive she would tell you so, too—she would know that I had never seen anyone like that picture.'

For an instant longer Alma's eyes held Marcia's, and then she turned away, saying quietly, 'Yes, I am sure Miss Cameron would have endorsed everything you say, but I shouldn't have believed her, any more than I believe you.'

'I can't help what you believe,' said Marcia sullenly, and it was the first time Alma had ever heard that clear youthful voice anything but dulcet. 'It's a badly done thing anyway, and I'm going to paint it out.'

She seized one of the brushes as she spoke, and with her back turned to Alma so that she was unable to see the portrait, she proceeded to splash dark paint all over the canvas. Only when the picture was obliterated did she turn round, but by then Alma had left her.

Alma's footsteps stumbled as she went down the stairs. She clutched at the hand-rail for support. It was surprising that she could keep her feet at all, it would have been easy to sway forward and fall headlong.

Somehow or other she reached the foot of the stairs, and feeling faint and sick she dragged herself to the drawing-room. A tremendous weariness hung weights on her arms, her feet, her eyelids. She felt as though she had been through a frightful storm, and without any other thought than that she must rest, she threw herself down on the settee, mechanically pulled a cushion under her head and was almost instantly asleep.

She was still asleep when presently Toni, followed by Richard, came through the long windows. At first Toni did not notice her, but then as her eyes went round the room and she saw that slight form cast down on the settee in an attitude which conveyed complete exhaustion, she uttered an exclamation and went over to her.

Richard divined her alarm and was astonished. 'She's only asleep.'

'Yes . . . but . . .'

The sentence was not completed for Alma stirred and sat up; she rubbed her eyes sleepily, took a moment to collect herself and then with a cry glanced at the clock. 'Oh, how dreadful of me! What on earth possessed me? I must have been asleep for more than three hours. I only lay down to rest for a minute . . . and now it's dinner time and I'm not even dressed. Toni darling, and this is Doctor Carlyn, of course, will you ever forgive me?'

Toni smiled. 'You must have been dreadfully tired to sleep so heavily. For a moment you frightened me . . . you looked as though you had gone far away.'

'Yes . . . I was tired,' Alma said, seeming to ignore the last words. But she thought that if she had not fallen into that stupefying sleep, she might well have gone out of her mind.

'I'll ring for drinks,' she said, 'and then I won't be more than two minutes changing my dress and tidying up generally. Louis should be in almost at once, but he had to see about something at The Red Towers.'

'Did Marcia go with him?' Toni asked.

'No—it was some technical point, it wouldn't have interested her.'

On the words the door opened and Marcia came in. Both Alma and Toni looked at her with astonishment, for it was not her habit to wear sophisticated gowns. The dress she was now wearing was black, and very smart. It had a long, flowing skirt, long sleeves and a high neck. The cuffs, collar and the border of the skirt were embroidered with silver sequins. Her corn-coloured hair was piled high and secured with a high silver comb. This style gave her distinction and height, and instead of looking younger than her twenty-two years she now looked older.

It was obvious from Richard's expression that this was not at all the type of young woman he had expected to see, as how could it be from Toni's written descriptions of her childishness and unworldliness? But when Marcia greeted him her innate simplicity became apparent. She said, 'Oh, you must be Dr Carlyn. I've wanted to meet you so much. I've pinned my faith to you, for I'm sure you will help me.'

She put out her hand to him, and Richard held it closely for a moment. It was a thin, nervous little hand and very cold. It gave him some clue to her temperament. He said gravely, 'That's partly why I came down. Toni has told me about your plans. Naturally they interest me very much. I have many patients who are insufficiently ill for hospital treatment but who have not been away for any sort of holiday for ten years or more. But most of them would have to be persuaded that this Home was quite unlike those to which hospital patients are usually sent. Most are excellent, but because they suggest rules and regulations, they are regarded with aversion.'

'I can understand that,' Marcia said. 'Rules are frightening. I hope there will be as few as possible. I want people to go to bed when they like and get up when they like, and they must have picnic meals outside, or meals in the house if they prefer. I want to have two or three carriages for their use, and the matron and the nurses must have elastic kind of minds, and remember that people can't get well or be happy unless they have freedom. I need that for myself, everyone needs it.'

'But Marcia,' Toni remonstrated, 'you do have as much freedom as any human being could have. Louis is constantly saying that if you do what pleases yourself, you also please him.'

Marcia's eyes were wistful as she turned her gaze to Toni. 'Some people are not born to freedom,' she observed.

During this conversation Alma had pressed the bell, and had given an order to Hetty, who now entered with bottles and glasses on a tray. Alma said, 'Please help yourselves to what you want. I must go and dress.'

Toni said, 'Can I have a glass of sherry and drink it in your room while you dress? Then Marcia and Richard can talk together, and perhaps get to know each other more quickly.'

Alma agreed. Toni noticed that she avoided looking at Marcia, had kept her eyes away from her since she had first joined them. She wondered and felt a slight premonition of trouble.

'Can one get to know people quickly?' Marcia said. 'Isn't it usually that one knows them immediately or never does? I know you very well already . . . but of course Toni has talked a lot about you.'

'Has she?' Richard was normally a self-contained young man, but it was impossible to keep the pleasure out of his voice, for it seemed to him that it was a good sign if Toni had made him the topic of conversation.

As though she guessed his thoughts, Marcia said, 'It isn't only that she has spoken about you in connection with the Home, because she thought you would help me, but also because you are one of her most interesting friends.' Then, rather disappointingly for Richard, she qualified this by saying: 'But doctors nearly always are interesting, because they know so many people and are interested in so many people.'

'Well, yes, that's the nature of our job, I suppose,' Richard agreed.

He watched her as she poured him a sherry and when he took the glass from her, he said, 'Tell me what you intend to do in this scheme of yours. I gather it will mean something more to you than supplying the money.'

'Oh, yes,' she agreed. 'It will mean much more than that. I want to make friends with the people. I want to make them happy. If any of them like me, I want to help them when they leave the Home. I want to do good.'

'That's a very fine ambition,' Richard said gently.

She looked squarely at him then, and there was grief and pain in her eyes. She said, 'You're religious, aren't you? Do you think God always makes a person pay if they have done anything unfair, anything wrong?'

Richard thought before he answered. 'Judging from what I've seen, people who do wrong generally have to pay for it, but that perhaps is more a law of nature than God's will. But,' he added as Marcia's head drooped, 'anyone who does a wrong thing can always be sorry and atone.'

'That's what I want to do,' she said eagerly. 'I thought if I gave up part of my life and a lot of my money, I might be able to put things right. I mean . . . the person who would suffer, who would pay, wouldn't be me . . . and I can't bear to think of that.'

Richard was silent for so long that Marcia said with apprehension, 'Do you think it won't do any good?'

He looked at her then with pity. Strange, truncated confessions were no novelty to him. He had long realized that because he was a doctor, confidences were thrust upon him by people who were naturally reserved and would never have thought of confiding in even their closest friends.

'I don't think any of us can make a bargain with God,' he said. 'And actually nobody ever does make a bargain with somebody they love.'

'But I don't love Him!' Marcia cried. 'He's cruel . . . He has been cruel to me. I have a lot to forgive . . . and I'm afraid . . .' She broke off and walked to the other end of the room. Standing with her back to him, looking out on the garden, she said, 'When Toni told me about you, and said you were coming to stay, I felt you would help me. But you can't unless I tell you everything, and that's so difficult, and Janet said I mustn't—not ever. But she's dead, and I must tell somebody. You . . . you would keep it secret if I did tell you, wouldn't you?'

'You know that.'

'Then . . . some day—while you're here . . . not this evening, there isn't the time.'

'Whenever you want to tell me, I'll be ready to listen,' Richard assured her.

'I don't know how I'm going to get through this evening. I can't look beyond it. I suppose everything may fall into proportion later, but at the moment . . .'

Alma ended with an eloquent gesture, one which suggested complete hopelessness, and Toni said, 'I felt there was something wrong when I saw you asleep. It was unlike you, and somehow you looked so broken. As though you had flung yourself down in absolute exhaustion.'

'So I had, but it was an exhaustion of the spirit. I've never known anything like it, it was as though I'd been battered, flailed until I was almost dead.'

There was a startling violence in Alma's voice. Toni, sitting on the side of the bed and sipping her sherry, watched her as she hurriedly changed into a dinner dress, and ran a comb through her silvery curls.

'But what happened?' Toni asked. 'I suppose it's something to do with Marcia?'

Alma's back was turned to her, but Toni could see her reflection in the mirror, could see the tense strain of her expression, the look in her eyes which was one of horror.

'Yes, it's to do with Marcia,' Alma agreed. 'Oh, Toni, there's something horribly wrong there. Oh, why had my poor boy to meet her and fall in love with her?'

She had said much the same thing before, but with a gentle regret and with her affection for Marcia still intact, but now there was a note of fear in her voice.

'What has she done?' Toni asked.

Alma, brush in hand, turned round to face her. 'There's so little time to tell you, I must hurry, and yet I can't wait—I *have* to tell you, Toni. Do you remember how I described the girl in the car who really wasn't there at all . . . that horrible, evil ghost of a girl?'

'Of course I remember. It's not the sort of story one would be likely to forget.'

'I'd come to believe,' Alma said, 'that the vision was nothing to do with Marcia, that it was some phenomenon of my own mind . . . a delusion, but now I know it wasn't. That girl exists, or did exist at some time. There was a canvas on Marcia's easel. She had covered it up, and without thinking I drew the cloth away. There was that horrible, triumphantly gloating, dark face looking at me. Marcia had painted it.'

'Alma, how extraordinary! Does Marcia know you have seen the painting?'

'She came back into the room while I was looking at it. She was violently agitated, and tore the cloth from my hand. She swore it was a face she had painted from her imagination. She said she had never known any such person—but she was lying. I'm convinced she was lying. She was terrified, taken quite out of herself by terror, and for a moment she wasn't at all the Marcia we know, so dreamy and smooth-tempered and gentle. Fright made her angry, and while I was still there she took up one of her brushes and began to daub paint all over the canvas, obliterating the picture. Oh, Toni, what am I to do?'

'Nothing; what can you do, unless you tell Louis, and he will probably ridicule the whole thing. If Marcia said she painted an imaginary face then he will believe her.'

'Yes, because he loves her, but all the same he isn't happy. How can he be? It isn't a normal marriage.'

Toni glanced at her and then glanced away. She asked, though she hated herself for asking, 'Do you mean—they are not lovers?'

'I am sure they are, but it must be like being in love with a shaft of moonlight. There's something inhuman about Marcia, I've always felt it. Haven't you?'

'I don't know . . . I agree there's something we don't understand about her.'

Alma uttered a deep sigh. She said, 'I have moments of bleak despair—wondering what his future will be, not seeing any future for him.'

'Surely that's exaggeratedly pessimistic.'

'Oh yes,' Alma acknowledged, 'by the light of reason it is. I've nothing definite to say against Marcia, I don't even *want* to say anything against her. I feel that she's as much a victim of her past, whatever it is, as Louis is a victim of his love for her. But there's no happiness for Louis with her, any more than there was for the knight-at-arms.'

'The knight-at-arms?'

'You know the poem "La Belle Dame Sans Merci", I often think it is so with him. Marcia has him in thrall, and there's something about her which is not ordinarily mortal.'

But this was too much for Toni, and she said so. Alma was letting her fancy run away with her. If she did not take care she would have a nervous breakdown. She spoke severely, because of a curious feeling of fright, of being out of her depth. She got up and, in a matter-of-fact way, hooked Alma's dress at the side, fastened the bangle with which her nervous fingers were playing, and arm in arm they went downstairs.

Louis had joined Richard and Marcia when they reentered the room, and for the rest of the evening the atmosphere was normal enough. Louis, having no idea that anything was amiss, helped to make it so. His eyes rested often upon his lovely wife and always with admiration. Toni thought that Marcia played up to him. She was more animated than usual.

The week-end guests were expected on the morrow, and the talk turned upon Virginia Challis, who was the most fascinating actress of her day; a mature woman with a grown-up son, though she looked no more than twenty-seven or eight. Marcia listened attentively, and asked several questions about her. Was she really so beautiful? Had Louis known her for a long time? Did he find her very attractive?

It was obvious that she was not only intrigued, but also a little jealous, and Toni wanted to laugh. Louis was not the type to fall in love with a woman old enough to be his mother, and it struck Toni as odd that Marcia, who was revealing that she could be jealous, should never have evinced the least jealousy of her. And in that she showed her wisdom, Toni thought with sudden bitterness; Louis since his marriage had scarcely been aware of her existence.

The party broke up about eleven o'clock and Toni and Richard drove home together. Toni, curious to know what kind of impression Marcia had made on him, said regretfully. 'I hoped you would have more time to talk to Marcia alone. There was little chance this evening of any private conversation.'

'But we had one, you know,' Richard said. 'You gave us the opportunity when you went upstairs with Mrs Dorman.'

'But that was for such a short time.'

'Much can be said in a short time. She understands me pretty well, I think, and I understand her a little.'

'Alma is worried about her, Richard. She has all sorts of queer fancies about Marcia. Some of them are completely wild, but one has to admit that she is baffling. You don't realize it at first, but when you think over what she has told you, it doesn't hang together too well.'

'She must have confided fully in her husband.'

'I don't think so. Louis adores her, but she's a mystery to him.'

'Isn't it an understood thing that all women are mysteries? If a woman can remain so to her husband she is the more desirable to him, I suppose.'

'Oh, Richard,' said Toni with exasperation, 'don't fence with me, and don't think I'm idly curious. I'm worried about that family. Alma and Louis are two of my oldest friends, and I've become fond of Marcia. It's impossible to treat her as a faerie child all her life, and at present she seems to have only one foot in this world.'

'And yet she is full of practical plans,' Richard said. 'This Home for instance.'

Toni said slowly, 'That in the beginning was inspired by generous pity. Marcia saw how the poor lived and it horrified her. But now I feel that she has lost sight of her original inspiration . . . she's positively eager to throw her money away, and Louis won't try to stop her, because he considers it's her own to do as she wishes with, and because he'd be better pleased if she had to depend on him. Once or twice I've felt that she was offering it all up as a sort of sacrifice, to propitiate something or someone.'

Although her shrewdness startled Richard, he made no direct comment, but as they alighted outside her home, he said, 'She's not a faerie child by any means, Toni, but a most unhappy girl, who needs all the kindness and sympathy her friends can give her.'

6

Cosmo Gallion came down by train to Devon. With ostentation he travelled second class, for to his friends Cosmo frequently remarked that luxury was a vulgarity, and unworthy of anyone who followed a creative profession. A few of his intimate friends might smile cynically, but the majority believed him, for he lived alone in a small flat in the unfashionable part of Kensington, wore shabby clothes, and so far as was known was not cursed by extravagant habits.

But the very few knew he was a gambler and an unlucky one. Horses which were considered a safe bet, and were heavily backed by Cosmo, invariably failed to stay the course; he had probably won less than a hundred pounds in the fifty-odd years of his life, whereas he must have lost several thousands. This and a connoisseur's taste for rare wines, were his secret and treasured vices, and had he sacrificed them, life would have been savourless.

At the moment, however, it seemed as though he might have to cut down on his extravagances, for he was heavily in debt, and although his salary as literary editor of a famous paper was large, it was mortgaged for several months ahead. The solution was to write another book, but although the only one he had written had proved lucrative, he was not creative by temperament. A historical novel was the only type within his compass, and that necessitated a considerable amount of research work. As Cosmo already believed himself to be overworked as a columnist, the outlook was not promising.

Although by no means a popular man, he was sought after, being in his way a celebrity, and it was rarely that he did not receive some kind of a week-end invitation, besides requests to dine and lunch during the week and often to fill the position of guest of honour at some literary function.

Driving down to Devon today, he reflected that if any more enticing invitation had arrived, even at the eleventh hour, he would have sent his specious excuses, for he was no lover of the country, and Louis Walters's invitation held out no particular promise.

It was true that he rather liked Louis, and considered his work promising. It was on the cards that one day he might be famous, in which case in one way or another he could probably be of use. After all, Cosmo told himself, one did well to take the long view. It was occasionally worth while to become the guide, philosopher and friend of a coming young man.

These reflections helped to induce a more mellow mood, until he actually alighted at Meadow House, when he frowningly observed Virginia Challis, accompanied by Alma and her tall son, saunter around the corner of the house.

He had known Virginia for many years and heartily disliked her, a dislike which she doubtless perceived, for she treated him with a ribald disrespect, and he had heard that at parties, at which he had not been present, she had given a most cruel impersonation of him in the act of delivering an extempore after-dinner speech. Cosmo was no orator and was apt to repeat himself unless his speech was carefully memorized beforehand. He had been told that Virginia's impersonations consisted of no more than three sentences, interspersed with coughs and hiccoughs. The latter was libel, he reflected, for he could hold his drink better than most men.

And now here was Virginia and her gawky son as fellow guests for the week-end. It was unpardonable of Louis. A host's first business was to find out if his guests were compatible.

Virginia in a cream wool dress was looking beautiful and young, and when she saw Cosmo her small nose wrinkled up as she smiled impertinently.

'Why look who's here!' she cried. 'Cosmo darling, the last time we were guests together, I must have been seven years old—no more, for I distinctly remember that when the others played tennis, I sat on your knee and was frightfully attracted because you had a lovely soft down all over your face. You must have been about due for your first shave.'

By means of this entirely imaginary story she had established the fact that Cosmo was at least ten years older than herself, which was not true. If anything, thought Cosmo indignantly, he was three or four years her junior. A humourless man, he did not suspect that Virginia was not speaking for the benefit of her audience but for sheer love of teasing. She was not in the slightest degree age-conscious, knowing that in appearance, vitality and outlook she was younger than most women in their early thirties.

'At that age,' Cosmo said coldly, 'I was in Canada. My mother was widowed early and went to live there with some relations, taking me with her. I first saw you, my dear Virginia, at the time of your third marriage, when you were not exactly in your first youth and this young man,' indicating Denis, 'was not born then.'

'How could he have been born as Ralph, my third husband, is his father? It's quite true,' she added, turning a dazzling smile on Alma who stood beside her, 'that I did not attempt maternity until I was getting on in years, which was courageous of me, don't you think, dear Mrs Walters? You must have been an infant when Louis was born.'

'I am only too glad for you to think so.' Alma laughed, though she was slightly dismayed. Evidently these two were old enemies, and although their bickering throughout the week-end might be amusing, Alma, confused and unhappy in her mind, longed for serenity.

What a pity that Louis had asked the lean-faced, bitter-looking man at the same time as Virginia. Alma took an instant dislike to Cosmo Gallion. His clothes, she thought, were ostentatiously shabby, for he could not possibly be poor. Cosmo was at the moment extracting a cigarette from his case, and Alma glanced distastefully away from his nicotine-stained fingers.

'You've had a long drive on this hot day,' she said. 'Do come into the house and have a drink. Louis will join us almost at once, he's showing his other guests, Mr Panfrey and his wife, their bedroom. They arrived only just before you. I dare say you already know them.'

Cosmo nodded. 'Yes, Panfrey and I are old acquaintances,' he said, 'though we haven't run across one another just lately.'

Actually the fact that James Panfrey had also been asked for the week-end made the long journey worthwhile. Panfrey was a literary agent who might possibly be induced to take an interest in Cosmo's new historical novel.

He followed Alma into the drawing-room, admiring her in a detached way. Marcia, who had been curled up in a corner of the sofa reading, looked up as they came in, and as she did so, Cosmo involuntarily stepped back. Although he was an accomplished poker-face, he could not wholly control the flash of incredulous surprise which flashed across his features. Alma noticed it and Marcia said, 'It's Mr Gallion, isn't it? I've been so anxious to meet you.'

She held out her hand to him and he took it in the loose, flaccid grasp which many people considered one of the most unpleasant things about him: 'Really? May I ask why?'

'For quite an ordinary reason. Ages ago I read your book *Sovereign Splendour*, and was enthralled by it. I've never forgotten it, and I was thrilled when my husband said he knew you, and that you would be coming to stay this week-end.'

'You are Louis's wife?' Cosmo seemed taken aback.

'Marcia didn't give me the chance to introduce you,' Alma said. 'But you knew Louis was married, didn't you?'

'Oh, yes, he told me so when he wrote. Is it too late to congratulate you both?'

'Of course not. Here is Louis now,' said Marcia.

The two men shook hands, but Cosmo's gaze wandered exploringly over Marcia's face and figure. Becoming restive under such an intent gaze, she flushed slightly and turned away, and then Cosmo said, 'I apologize. I was staring at you, but the fact is you remind me of someone I once knew very well, but whom I've not met for years. When I walked in here and you got up from the sofa, it was like coming face to face with her again . . . though of course she must be middle-aged by now.'

Marcia said with interest and no embarrassment, 'How queer! They say everyone has their double somewhere, and perhaps I am hers.'

Cosmo shook his head. His eyes were still fixed on her, as though the fascination was so strong he could not look away.

'No—the likeness is not so exact as that,' he said. 'It's the colouring, and your eyes . . . something about your expression.'

Virginia sauntered in through the window, and exclaimed with pleasure when she saw the tray of drinks.

'Darling,' she entreated, 'if you have Angostura and gin,

there's no short drink that I like better.'

'Easily supplied,' Alma said. 'Perhaps you'd like to mix it yourself.'

Louis, having greeted Cosmo formally, told him that Panfrey had been delighted to know he was there, and that he would be down immediately. The two men stood by the window, drinks in hand, while the women were grouped together, talking.

'You have a very beautiful wife,' Cosmo said. 'I was just telling her that she reminds me of an old friend, but I hardly suppose there's any relationship.'

'I wonder. Marcia was a Miss Norman.'

Cosmo's face betrayed nothing. He shook his head, as though in disappointment.

'It doesn't ring a bell?' Louis inquired.

'No. A pity! I thought there might be some relationship and I should have been interested to have had news of my old friend.'

With the entrance of George Panfrey and his wife, who was young and pretty and gay, the conversation became general.

Lena Panfrey had remembered Cosmo as a cynically amusing companion, but she complained afterwards to her husband that he had become strangely dull. He had left all the conversation to her, and seemed to be in a dream.

As a fact, Cosmo was, and Marcia was the centre of the dream.

Rita's daughter! But it didn't make sense. Could Rita have had another child after he had left her? But no, this girl was twenty-two or more . . . he had heard her allude casually to her twenty-first birthday. And that was right enough—both the girls would be in their twenty-third year by now. It was with difficulty he repressed a shudder.

But if he was right, and he must be right, what on earth had happened? He was consumed with curiosity, but praised himself for his swift denial that the name of Norman struck any chord of remembrance. His first instinctive thought had been that it would be confoundedly awkward if the truth were known, but now other thoughts were pressing on him. It occurred to him that, far from being an unprofitable week-end, this might be one of lucrative possibilities.

The party that evening was a festive one. Richard and Toni arrived just as Gladys, who had been pressed into service and had, under Alma's supervision, cooked a very good meal, announced that dinner was served.

Toni was relieved that the tension of which she had been so conscious of late had dispersed. Alma looked serene, and Marcia was more animated than usual. She sat beside Cosmo Gallion, and it was evident to those who knew him that he was making a special effort to charm and interest her.

It was a sight which confounded Virginia, who had never before seen Cosmo put himself out for anyone, unless for a very good cause. She could not imagine that this young wife of Louis's, lovely and unusual though she was, could be of the least benefit to him, unless he planned to make a long stay here at Marcia's request. But would the quiet peace and beauty of Devon and Meadow House hold any particular appeal for such as Cosmo?

Marcia listened with keen interest as Cosmo described how he had come to write *Sovereign Splendour*, the book which had enthralled her. Actually he had almost forgotten the state of his mind at that time, though he vaguely remembered that the research had been tedious in the extreme. But it was easy to invent incidents, to pretend to a sense of inspiration which he had never possessed. By the end of the meal Marcia felt as though she had known him for years, which was the effect at which he had aimed.

It made it easy to detach her afterwards from the others, to suggest a stroll round the garden.

'What about walking through the orchard?' Cosmo suggested. 'We shall be well away from the house there and can talk. I've something to say to you.'

Unconsciously his voice had changed, all the charm had vanished from it, and Marcia looked up at him in surprise.

'Something important?' she asked.

'Yes.' There was a bench under the apple trees, and he seated himself and signed to Marcia to do the same. He said abruptly, 'I know who you are.'

'Who I am?'

'You'd better prepare yourself for a shock, my dear. Your mother was Rita Norman, and she was my wife.'

Marcia's face was blank, positively stupid with astonishment. She stared at him, her eyes wide, her mouth a little open.

'It's the truth,' he said flatly.

After a prolonged silence Marcia found her voice. 'Do you mean that you are my father?'

'So I suppose.'

'But it can't be. His name was Norman.'

'So was mine originally. I changed it by deed poll years ago, when an uncle who left me money made the condition that I should take his name.'

'I can't believe it . . . I mean it's hard to believe,' Marcia murmured. 'I know nothing about you . . . you might have been dead. Mamma told us nothing.'

'Ah!' He pounced on this. 'Does the We mean you and Monica?'

'Yes. Did you know about us?' The words left her lips reluctantly.

'I saw you both a few months after you were born. Your mother and I quarrelled, when she was in her early pregnancy. She was a cold, obstinate woman, but beautiful. I was very much in love with her but she was proud of herself and proud of her money, I had no share in it, and she insisted on living in the country, which I loathed. We finally parted. I had no idea she was expecting a child, and after many months when the memory of her beauty pulled me back to her, I came down to see her unexpectedly, and found you both.'

'Was that the end of—of your wish to be her husband again?' Marcia said in a faint voice.

'It was.'

'I suppose you were—ashamed.'

'You suppose wrongly. For God's sake, what was it to do with me? You were your mother's children . . . it was a curse on her she thought, because she had given up her religion, turned her back on it.'

'Was she religious?' Marcia asked.

'She was a Catholic . . . she came of an old, devout family. The lord only knows what kink got into her, when she threw over the traces. At the time I knew her, she had nothing but bitterness for all the revealed religions . . . and then this happened to her.'

'It didn't turn her back to God. Anything I learnt, I learnt from Janet, who was a Dissenter. I was interested. I tried to believe, and I tried to forgive God for what He had done to—us. But now it seems that it was my mother I should have tried to forgive.'

He shrugged. 'Look on it as you wish. Your guess as to why such a thing had to happen is as good as mine.'

After a moment Marcia said abruptly, 'I must be very like my mother, as she was when a girl, otherwise you wouldn't have recognized me. Monica was not at all like her—or like me.'

'What has happened to Monica?' Cosmo asked.

'She is dead. So is Mamma. There was a landslip, and we were all carried away with a part of the cliff. When we were found, they were dead, but I was alive, and they saved me. I was in a nursing home for months; there was one big operation which saved my life, and others afterwards. I don't remember anything. I was very ill and unconscious.'

'Does your husband know about Monica?' Cosmo asked.

Although he was burningly anxious to discover this, his voice was cool and unconcerned. He had no intention of frightening Marcia into telling a lie.

'No . . . I was afraid to tell him, and Janet advised me not to.'

'Janet? Oh, you mean some servant or attendant you had?'

'She was our governess and companion. I loved her, but Monica didn't. When the others died, she stayed with me. When I was strong enough we travelled . . . in Scotland and Ireland and after that abroad. It was in Spain that I met Louis and we fell in love. We were married very quickly, because Janet knew she was ill, and wanted me to have a protector. She died soon afterwards.'

'Did Rita leave you comfortably off?' Cosmo asked.

'Oh, yes, everything she had came to me. It's far too much. I'm using some of it to launch a convalescent home for sick people—women and girls who need special care, and special treatment.'

'Good lord, surely you realize there are sufficient institutions of that kind already?'

Cosmo was really indignant, and showed it. He could not imagine a more wanton waste of money. What in the world was Louis about to allow such reckless squandering?

'This won't be an institution, it will be quite different. It will be a tremendous interest to me. Dr Carlyn has promised to help me.'

'But my dear girl, it's absurd. With as much money as you appear to possess you will never lack for interests. I assure you that amateur philanthropy is the most unsatisfactory enterprise you could have hit upon. If your bent lies towards charity, why not help individual people who are in need of it?'

'But I don't know any individual people who need help. I scarcely know anyone at all.'

It was the opening for which Cosmo had hoped. He said with a short laugh, 'There's one needy individual to whom I can at once introduce you—me!'

'You!'

'I don't bleat about my troubles to all the world, Marcia, but as a fact I'm embarrassingly hard up. A gift of a few thousands would be uncommonly useful, and to whom should you hand out money, if not to your father? If Rita had had any sense of fairness, she would have left me at least a share of her fortune.'

Marcia turned to look at him. He was surprised and somewhat disconcerted by the steady appraisal of her grey eyes which were no longer dreamy. He was even more surprised when she said, 'I owe you nothing, and neither did my mother. You deserted her and you never took the least interest in us—you had no pity for us--you were only disgusted, and you left my mother to bear everything alone. I can't think why you have told me you are my father—it couldn't have been because you had any wish to claim me as a daughter. You would have been horrified and disgusted if Monica were still alive.'

Cosmo fought down his cold anger and answered mildly, 'Wouldn't that have been natural? But it's difficult to remember Monica when I see you as you are now. You are a lovely young woman, of whom any father might be proud. If you wish it, I am perfectly ready to acknowledge you before all the world.'

The blood rushed to Marcia's cheeks. Deliberately she drew herself away from him. She said coldly, 'But I don't wish it. You may not be ashamed to acknowledge me as a daughter, but I should certainly be ashamed to acknowledge you as a father.'

Cosmo could not have been more astonished had she hit him across the face. For a moment he could not speak for anger, and then he said, 'I make a bad enemy, my dear, but have it that way, if you wish.'

'I'm not afraid,' she replied coldly.

'But are you wise to be so fearless? As you have not told your husband your past history, and Monica's, you evidently don't wish him to know of it. In fact you told me only a few minutes ago that you had lacked the courage to tell him.'

Now as she realized the threat in his words, and realized too the menace he could be to her, Marcia's heart started to pound wildly, but she said, 'You wouldn't dare to tell him; if you did it would show you up in a very bad light. You behaved vilely to my mother—and to us.'

'Your husband's opinion of me is not important, but it won't be necessary to acquaint him personally with the facts. An anonymous letter, a telephone conversation in a disguised voice, would certainly start him wondering, and he would no doubt make some inquiries which would open up the whole matter and eventually expose it.'

'You couldn't . . . it would be such a vile thing to do.'

'I certainly could, for the simple reason that it wouldn't seem vile to me. People, you know, can always justify their actions, and I should justify mine by the belief that it is a wrong thing for young wives to deceive their husbands, and extremely culpable of them to acknowledge no filial duty to a father.'

Marcia gasped and was silent. She sat with her hands clenched in her lap, staring before her. Darkness filled her soul. Cosmo glanced at her and decided not to break the silence at once. It was only when she got up and moved away from him that he put out his hand and grasped her arm.

'Now, be sensible,' he urged. 'If you behave in a reasonable manner, I shan't upset your life in any way. I have far too little money and you have far too much. In my opinion I'm entitled to share your good fortune, and it's perfectly simple for you to give me a comfortable income.'

She asked with her face averted, 'What do you consider a comfortable income?'

'Let us say a couple of thousand a year—come, that's not too hard on you. It will cost you ten times as much to run your Home.'

'I won't do it,' Marcia cried. 'I hate you . . . you can starve for all I care.'

There was a passionate vehemence in her voice which nobody who knew her had ever heard. She looked at him with such a depth of black hatred that he was startled, and even for a moment aghast.

'I shan't starve,' he said smoothly. 'But you, my dear, will probably become one more woman floating around the world, separated for some unknown reason from her husband.'

'I don't believe it. It would be a shock to Louis, but he would get over it.'

'He certainly might, he would probably pity you, but the natural happiness of your marriage would be ruined. You would doubt. There wouldn't be a day of your life in which you wouldn't question his love . . . you would see revulsion in his eyes, even when it wasn't there. Probably he hopes for children, but once he knew your history he would hope no more.'

She turned upon him then with panic. 'But there's no reason why I shouldn't have children . . . it—it isn't hereditary.'

He shrugged. 'Isn't it? You may be right. I'm not physician, and such speculations are outside my sphere, but speaking as a layman I should say that there was always the element of doubt.'

'Oh God, oh God!'

The cry was wrung from the very depths of Marcia's heart. She covered her face with her hands and sobbed. Cosmo watched her with indifference. Her contempt and her hatred had roused him to a cold anger. She might provide him with a substantial income, and he had no doubt that she would, but that would not soften him to her. He had put a thought into her mind which would breed poison there. She would never be able to forget it.

Marcia's sobs died down and she said, 'You shall have the money, but you must give me a few days. I shall have to get it from my lawyers. They have only just made arrangements for me to buy The Red Towers . . . I don't understand about investments, but some have had to be realized. I think the best thing would be for you to meet me in London next week, after I have seen my lawyers. They knew my mother was separated from her husband, and that he might be still alive. If I tell them I have discovered who my father is, and want to make him an allowance, it will seem natural enough, I suppose, though they will probably think the sum you mention is far too much.'

'You will persuade them it is not too much,' Cosmo said. 'You may even have to supplement it from time to time, for as you know the cost of living is high.'

Marcia's eyes were downcast, veiled by her long lashes. She was afraid to look up, because she knew that if she did, the flaming hatred in her heart would be revealed. So this was to be the way of it. Even two thousand a year would not be sufficient to buy her security; again and again she would have to find money for this horrible man. In her ears a voice seemed to whisper: 'But you won't do it—you won't be such a fool. It's blackmail, and if you give in to it, you'll be in bondage for the rest of your life.' She listened despairingly. Her heart cried: 'But what can I do? I can't keep my happiness unless I do what he wants.' But the voice in her mind, which was Monica's voice, had an answer to this: 'We can find a way. I'll show you a way.'

Marcia did not dare to think what this meant, but the voiceless message gave her a sense of strength. She said in a cool, a strangely gentle voice, 'I will do my best, but as I said you must allow me a little time, though for your own sake, I hope you will think better of it.'

'For my own sake?'

'It won't do you any good, however much money you get out of me. It can only do you harm. I could forget all this if you would.'

Cosmo laughed with genuine amusement. He said, 'The last thing I intend to do is to forget.'

She sighed. 'Very well then, but you will be sorry for it.'

'I can take care of that.'

She looked down at his hand which still grasped her arm. She said, 'Can I go now, please? We have been here a long time, and they will be wondering what has happened to us. Somehow or other we have to get through this week-end and behave as though there is nothing between us.'

'That's agreed,' Cosmo said. 'You need not fear that I shall betray you.'

'I know that. You will be careful for your own sake.'

There was no expression in her eyes as they briefly rested on him. She had banished all open evidence of distress as she had banished hatred. But when they walked back to the house together and his body casually brushed hers, her flesh crept with loathing. Such a man was not fit to live, she thought. He had broken her mother's life, and now he would break hers. He could not be of the least value to the world, and to anyone who came in intimate contact with him he would bring despair.

7

'How much longer do you intend to keep the breakfast going for Dr Carlyn?' asked Stella Benham disagreeably.

It was a commentary on the lack of friendliness between Richard and Stella that she always addressed him and spoke of him formally. As a general rule she was on Christian name terms with people after the briefest acquaintanceship.

Richard had not voiced the slightest criticism of her, but she suspected that he was full of unuttered criticism. He had spent a good deal of time with her husband and must suspect that Stella gave up little of her time to him.

It annoyed Stella when he unobtrusively relieved Toni of a few of her duties. He probably thought she was 'put upon' which was absurd. Being a trained nurse, it was natural for Toni to look after her father. Nevertheless there was something in Richard's quiet gaze when it rested on Stella which made her restive.

He was dull, too, she reflected discontentedly, he never joked with her or paid her compliments, and she would be thankful when his fortnight's visit was over. He was evidently attracted to Toni and what use was there in that? As though she would ever consent to marry a doctor with a ghastly East End practice. Why, it would mean living in Bethnal Green or wherever it was that he did live. Besides, there was the difference in religion. That would never do, Stella told herself; mixed marriages were rarely a success. It irritated her profoundy to see Toni 'spoiling' a guest who was not there at her invitation, and she had no scruples in saying so.

'I'm glad Richard can sleep late,' Toni now said mildly. 'He looked worn out when he arrived. His eyes were so tired, and I don't suppose he often has a long, restful night when he's at home. He is constantly called out at all hours.'

'Oh, well, that's his job,' Stella said. 'If he's as clever as you say, I don't know why he doesn't practise in a better district. Any dud doctor would do for those East End people—they're the scum of the earth, anyway.'

Toni looked angry, which did not often happen, but before she had time to reply, Richard came in.

He apologized for being late, saying with a smile that it must be the country air which made him sleep so long and so soundly, that and the blessed knowledge that there was no night bell to arouse him. Toni said she would make fresh coffee and that bacon and eggs wouldn't take a minute to cook. She would do it herself as the maids were busy.

Richard insisted on accompanying her to the kitchen, where the cook, who had been up to Everard Benham's room for his tray, soon joined them. She was an elderly and not ordinarily sweet-tempered woman, but the sight of Richard scrambling eggs in the frying pan and leaping away every time the fat spluttered, was too much for her, and she laughed, as she said later, until her sides ached.

Having had her laugh, she insisted on finishing the cooking of Richard's belated breakfast, and in the dining-room, which Stella had now left, he was soon enjoying it, while Toni sat opposite to him with a cup of coffee.

'You're too good to me,' he said. 'I've not had such a holiday as this for years, and I shall never forget it.'

'I wish I could think you would come down here next year, and that everything would be the same,' Toni said, 'but I'm afraid that Father . . .'

She broke off, and Richard said gently, 'He'll have gone by then, Toni, but who could want him to stay longer, in pain and so handicapped? He's such a good chap and so patient, but it can't be easy for him however much you love him.'

'I know,' Toni said. 'I try to think that way, but he's all I've got. I don't know what will happen to this place after his death. He has probably left it to Stella, and she will sell it I suppose. Her idea of bliss is a West End flat.'

'You wouldn't want to live on here either, would you?'

Richard asked. 'The first day I was here, you spoke of wanting to help me with my work. Were you serious?'

'Oh, yes, I was certainly serious, but I'm not sure if it would be a happy thing for you.'

'I am sure. There would be no strings attached. I've always said that unless you could love me there would be no happiness for either of us in marriage.'

'That's so true. But I'm awfully fond of you, my dear, and I admire you more than anyone I know. Isn't that a kind of love, even if it is not being *in* love?'

'Have you ever been in love, Toni?' Richard asked, and he did not look at her as he spoke.

'Yes—but it's over. It seems as though all that wanting, all that sadness and disappointment happened to a person who was not me. My life is not hampered by it any more.'

'I'm glad, my dear, but what a fool he was if he didn't love you.'

'You only think that because you are in love with me yourself. I'm terribly grateful to you, Richard, but it doesn't seem as sad for you as it would be for a different type of man. I mean you have so much without love. Your work, your Faith, your confidence in yourself. I always feel that you know all the answers.'

He said with astonishment, 'But that's not true. I ask few questions and so I don't look for the answers. You see, I believe that God knows what He is doing and therefore no tragedy—and I see enough tragedies—seems completely futile and wantonly cruel.'

'Then even if I never marry you, you will find a reason for it?'

'I hope so, but it will be hard.'

Toni said discontentedly, 'You have so much in your life without me. I should only be a kind of afterthought.'

'My dear girl, that's nonsense and you know it. Life goes on for many a man or woman who has lost a leg, or an arm—they mostly manage to do useful work, but do they ever forget they are maimed, that they could do a thousand times better and be a thousand times happier if their lost limb could be restored to them? I shall never be completely whole without you.'

Toni got up and walked over to the window. After a short silence, she said, 'Give me time. I'm not sure of myself but one day I may be. And—when I am free and can leave here, I'd be glad to work for you. I could do secretarial work and dispensing. I could act as an extra nurse. I should be there always to fill an odd job.'

'It would be wonderful to have you.'

Richard's cup was empty, and Toni re-filled it with coffee and said as she did so, 'What would you like to do this morning? It's going to be a fine day, and this afternoon, if you remember, we said we would drive into Seacrest with the party at Meadow House to look over The Red Towers. There are workmen now all over the place.'

'I fancy your little friend is avoiding me,' said Richard.

'Marcia avoiding you? But why should she?'

'I haven't an idea, unless it is that she was too confidential with me on our first meeting and now regrets it. People often react that way.'

'I shouldn't have thought they would with you. You're so thoroughly to be trusted; you're sympathetic and yet in a way detached, and one would always feel that you would try to do your best for anyone. Besides, Marcia was so anxious for your help and advice.'

'Well, she may be again, and if so, it's hers for the asking,' he said, and having finished his second cup of coffee got up from the table. 'I'll help your father to get dressed and into his chair, and then I'll get him out into the garden and read to him.'

'It's awfully sweet of you. It has been so stimulating for Father to have you here. He has had to put up with me for months.'

Richard smiled. 'Well, I don't think that was such ill fortune,' he replied, and as he passed her, he put his hand on her shoulder, and kept it there for a moment.

Left alone, Toni, although she had plenty of things to do, sat in silence for a while. Thoughts crowded in on her—and doubts and hopes. At this minute she was nearer to Richard than she had ever been. If she had not met Louis when she returned from America, if she had not been so constantly thrown in contact with him, the friendship with Richard might have ripened into love.

Certainly she had frequently thought of him while living in New York; she had admired and respected him, and had been interested in the progress of his career. But although she had known that he loved her, it had seemed to her to be a love incidental to his life. Also there had been the obstacle of religion. Toni's creed was nebulous, but the humane instincts were strong in her, she loved goodness for its own sake and this still seemed to her to be enough. She had not been antagonized by Richard's quiet conviction that it was not. But now, dimly, as through breaking clouds, she began to see that her natural love for life and beauty and goodness could be amplified by love and belief in a Divine Power.

A matrimonial conversion! Many a time this phrase had forced itself upon her with a wry flavour. She did not think highly of such conversions; she did not suppose that, in the main, the Catholic Church thought highly of them either. One could not change one's accepted philosophy or one's accepted religion as one might change the dress one happened to be wearing. Love of a human being alone could not alter one's convictions.

She moved restlessly, aware of her ignorance, of her uncertainty. She thought: 'It would take me ages and ages, I couldn't rush into such a thing as this. It would be frightful to make a mistake, to feel when it was too late that one preferred the old ways, and anyway I'm not sure if I love Richard entirely. It was such a short time ago that I wanted Louis.'

She was aware, as she thought of Louis, of a deep sorrow for him. He was unhappy and she could not see any lifting of his unhappiness. It was Marcia's strangeness and her beauty and her other-worldliness which had drawn him to her, but were such qualities enough?

Toni sighed and suddenly realized that although it was a saintly thing to yearn for Louis's happiness, as she did yearn, yet as she was by no means a saint she would, if she had still loved him, have experienced a satisfaction that after all Marcia was not all-sufficient for him. It was because her relationship to him had fallen into another pattern that she could be truly grieved for him.

This was a chastening thought and she sighed. What a muddle one's emotional contacts became! One longed to be simple and free and honest, and one might think one was until the flashing truth suddenly broke upon one.

The maid came in to clear the breakfast table, and it was a relief to have her thoughts dispersed. She got up and went out into the kitchen to see the cook and plan the meals for the day.

Three carriages took the party from Meadow House to Seacrest that afternoon, and Richard and Toni followed in another one. They set off rather late, and when they arrived at The Red Towers it was to find that Louis and Alma and Marcia with their guests were already there.

No workmen were to be seen and Toni was amused because Marcia said in a pleased voice that there had been some dispute and the men were threatening to strike.

'But you want the job finished, don't you?' Louis said.

'Of course I do,' Marcia agreed, 'but it won't be much of a delay. The foreman said the trouble would probably be settled by tomorrow, so it won't matter much and meanwhile we have the place to ourselves and can go over it without being worried by people trying to give us information about what hasn't been done and what still has to be done.'

Louis knew that this particular foreman had always been full of information when Marcia set foot in the building, but he rather sympathized with the man, because he guessed that he admired Marcia for her beauty, and took pleasure in being able to speak to her. He remembered how a few months ago he had been enchanted by that lovely, childish, dreamy face of hers, and with a shock realized that that first charmed perplexity had changed to disappointment. It was as though he had sought entrance to a room locked against him, had promised himself that behind that locked door there were all the treasures of the earth, and that when at last it had opened to him he had found it, if not precisely empty, yet furnished with such things as were of no value to him.

As the simile occurred to him he was ashamed, he accused himself of disloyalty. Marcia loved him, of that he had no doubt; she was sweet and compliant, she made few demands on him, but she was strange and alien, and hers was a secret soul which he could not penetrate. To him Marcia had typified romance, but now he knew that a man was not wise to wed for romance alone. He looked at Toni as she stood there with Marcia on one side of her and Richard Carlyn on the other, and, realizing the sanity, the sweetness of her, his heart swerved in regret. She was the woman he should have married. What a fool he had been, and how ruthlessly he had treated her. She had been so near loving him, but that love had withered as a flower withers when it is nipped by frost. But Toni's heart was large and generous and it would put forth fresh flowers, though not for him.

These were rending thoughts to tear the heart of any man, and Louis's heart was torn, though he showed no sign of pain. He led the way with Marcia through the empty rooms, pointing out all the alterations which they had planned. Already many of the interior walls had been demolished, some in order to make the living-rooms larger, some because it was necessary to let in windows which would look out upon the sea.

Virginia was especially interested and full of generous praise for Marcia. This Home when it was completed would be wonderful for those who were sick and weary. Was it to be entirely for people who lived in the East End? she asked Marcia, who looked vague and said she hadn't considered. It was to be a Home for women, but her original intention had been that it should be open for anyone who wanted sanctuary, peace and rest.

'In that case,' said Virginia, 'it seems to me that out-of-work, small-part actresses who never earn much money and are often tired to death would look upon it as heaven. I have many friends struggling to keep afloat, and lots of them are not young. Do keep a couple of rooms at least for poor players, Marcia, and I promise you they will be always occupied. My people would mix in quite well with Dr Carlyn's patients—actresses are not snobs whatever else they may be.'

'There's the snobbery of sickness,' Richard said, smiling. 'The person who has come through the most, generally considers himself superior to all others.'

As they explored the rambling old house, the party became scattered. Cosmo Gallion, who had stalked round in gloomy silence, for he could only think of the frightful waste of money, which this benevolent scheme would entail, eventually managed to fall in at Marcia's side. He put his hand on her arm and steered her towards a small room which the rest of the party had already looked in upon.

It was a room with two doors, and Marcia, determined to ignore the events of the night before, said conversationally, as though to a complete stranger, 'That door is to be walled up. It leads to one of the towers, and the turret rooms which are octagonal in shape and very small, won't be suitable for occupation—also the stairs leading up to them are far too twisting and steep for anyone to climb who isn't in the best of health.'

'Might as well have a look at it,' Cosmo said.

He opened the door and climbed the winding staircase, and after a moment's hesitation Marcia followed him. It was a giddy climb as he admitted when they had reached the small turret room. Marcia did it easily enough, but Cosmo was out of condition and his breath was coming heavily.

'There's a good view from the window,' Marcia said, but Cosmo was not interested in views and said so. He had come up here deliberately, intending to detach Marcia from the crowd.

'I've been thinking over our conversation last night,' he said, 'as I suppose you have.'

'I've tried not to think of it. As I explained I can do nothing until I have seen my solicitors, and that won't be possible until next week at the earliest.'

'It would be better for you to write to them and prepare them for your instructions. On thinking it over, I've decided that those had better be altered. It would be more to my advantage to have a lump sum, say thirty thousand pounds. Although you are young, nobody can guarantee how long you will live, and even I could not prevent you from making a will in which no provision would be made for my annuity. Thirty thousand pounds will be enough for me, for quite a time.'

'I won't do it,' Marcia said. 'For one thing my lawyers would do everything possible to dissuade me; they would even go to the length of consulting Louis. They would think I was out of my mind. Besides, the upkeep of this Home will take a large slice out of my capital and reduce my income by half.'

'That won't make so much difference to you as you suppose. The Inland Revenue would take much of your income in any case. Don't be a fool, Marcia, you know perfectly well your happiness is in my hands. What is the loss of a lump of money in comparison?'

'It wouldn't be the last lump sum of money you would expect from me.'

'As to that, I'm making no promises. Now listen to me; if you are obstinate, not only Louis but the whole world will know just what you are. I am a newspaper man and I can get the fullest publicity. An article by my pen describing the sensational events in your life would be front-page news, and would bring me a nice little sum which would be some compensation if I'm to be deprived of a share in your fortune, part of which is, as I contend, morally mine. That would be pleasant for Louis, wouldn't it? It would be pleasant for his sensitive, aristocratic mother, and grand news for all their friends!'

'Don't!' exclaimed Marcia, quivering.

'Well, it's in your own hands.'

She turned to look at him, and for a second he flinched. Her eyes did not look like Marcia's eyes, which were usually so serene and dreamy . . . now they were dark, threatening, and coldly warning. Her face also seemed to have darkened and changed.

'Yes—it's in my hands,' she said.

'I hope that means you intend to be sensible.'

'I haven't any choice. I hope you know what you are doing to yourself.'

'Doing to myself?'

'It means self-destruction, for you.'

Although he wanted to laugh caustically, he could not with that dark gaze fixed upon him, but he said, 'Surely you're not sufficiently absurd to think such evangelistic stuff will have any effect on me?'

Marcia laughed, quite gently, but it was such an unpleasant and eerie sound that involuntarily he glanced around, as though it had been a laugh uttered by a third person. When his gaze returned to her face, it was grave, almost he would have said regretful, and then instantaneously fear flashed over it, and this he welcomed, for fear of him made her his servant.

'I'm sure that nothing I can say will have any effect on you,' she said. 'You will have your own way.'

He nodded. 'I'm glad you've grasped that at last. You will write to your solicitors then, this evening or tomorrow?'

'Very well.'

He smothered his sigh of relief. For a moment he had known a curious doubt, some sixth sense had warned him of danger, but this he now dismissed as absurd. Marcia, leaning against the narrow window ledge, was limp and listless, her head down-bent, her cheeks pale. In spite of her spurt of rebellion it had been easy enough to subdue her.

He said, 'Now that's settled, we may as well continue the tour, but if you take my advice you will re-sell as soon as possible, for it seems pretty clear that you won't be able to afford to keep such a place going.'

He opened the door which led on to the winding staircase and started the laborious descent.

The remainder of the party explored the house thoroughly; they were galvanized to a more than ordinary interest by Virginia's enthusiasm. She was given to easy enthusiasms, but was not the less impelling for that, for the tide of her vitality carried the others along with her.

There never had been a more suitable house in which to recover from the storms and afflictions of the workaday world, so Virginia enthused. Every window, when the house was reconstructed, would look out upon a lovely scene, for the picturesque garden would be as delightful as the vista of sea and rocks, and stretch of golden sands. What a wonderful way Marcia had chosen to spend her money! Surely Louis must be terribly proud of her.

Alma, although she was charmed by Virginia as were all the others, found her attention wandering. She felt chilled and depressed and over her spirit there was gradually creeping the misty sense of fear and depression which was no new thing to her.

There was nothing at all to warrant the vague oppression; everyone except herself was gay and seemingly carefree, even Louis, who had, she knew, been far from happy of late. She glanced round her uneasily and asked, 'Where did Marcia and Mr Gallion go? They've been away for a long time.'

'Looking at some other part of the house, I suppose,' Louis said. 'I'll call them.'

He raised his voice and the name 'Marcia' echoed stridently through the empty rooms. For a moment as the echoes died away there was no reply, and then they heard a faint cry, which a second later was followed by one terrifying scream after another.

Louis, with an exclamation, rushed out of the room and down the stairs, heading for the other wing, and after a moment of stunned silence his guests followed him. Alma went laggingly. She was not so much terrified, as struck by a sense of doom.

Louis was the first to reach the turret stairs, and there he came to an abrupt standstill, but he stretched out his hand behind him to ward off the others. The broken body of Cosmo Gallion lay at his feet. He had fallen in an unsightly twisted position, and his eyes looked up at Louis. He was not dead and his lips moved soundlessly.

Louis bent over him and Richard at his elbow said, 'Close the door . . . the others mustn't come in.'

But Alma was already standing within the door. The others had made room for her when she came up with them, for she had been imperious when she pushed her way though the clustering group. Now, very white and trembling violently, she stood staring upwards, unable to tear her eyes away from the dark, smiling face of the girl who hung over the stair-rail. The mocking eyes looked back at her, amused, satisfied, because Alma was aware of her, though the others were not. To them the evil creature was invisible. She was not of this world. Again, as on the first time when Alma had seen the dark girl, her face and figure faded out; became shadowy and then not there at all. Alma herself was in her son's arms.

'Marcia . . . what has happened to Marcia?' she cried.

'I'll look after Marcia . . . don't worry,' Louis soothed her. 'Take the others away, and I'll be with you as soon as I can.'

He pushed her gently through the open door and into Toni's arms, and went back to Richard who, kneeling, looked up at Louis and said, 'He's dead. The fall broke his back.'

Louis scarcely heard him, scarcely glanced at the dead man. He went quickly up the stairs to the turret room. Marcia stood pressed against the wall, her hands spread out on either side of her, her eyes fixed and blank.

'He fell, I heard him fall,' she said. 'I couldn't help it . . . I couldn't save him.'

'Dear, of course you couldn't save him. We said from the first that those stairs were dangerous and he must have missed his footing. Dr Carlyn is with him now—everything possible will be done . . .'

'But you can't do anything . . . you mustn't,' Marcia wailed. 'It's better he should be dead, and she knew it. That's why she killed him.'

Louis held her off and looked into her eyes. 'What do you mean? Who killed him?'

'Monica . . . She has always protected me and this was the only way.'

'Marcia,' cried Louis urgently, 'what are you saying?'

She gave a long deep sigh. She said in a voice of utter, despairing surrender, 'I can't keep it to myself, not any longer. I shall have to tell you. She's part of me . . . but that's not my fault, I longed to be free.'

Louis could make no sense of the broken words, as

Marcia sighed and fell limply against him.

Neither Alma nor Louis ever forgot the nightmare hours which followed. The police were called, while Marcia still lay unconscious on the floor of the turret room. Everyone was questioned, but eventually Cosmo Gallion's body was borne off in an ambulance, and Marcia, partially recovered, was taken back to Meadow House.

Virginia and her son and the Panfreys would have departed for London that night, feeling their presence was an anxiety to Alma, but the police insisted that nobody was to leave the house until there had been opportunity for further investigation.

Everyone who had been at The Red Towers was questioned again that evening, but as it was obvious that nobody but Marcia had been near Cosmo Gallion at the time of his fall, they were told that if it was their wish they could leave on the morrow. It was impossible to question Marcia, for she was unconscious, Richard having given her a sedative which had sent her into a heavy sleep.

The local police, who knew Alma and Louis, were sympathetic and considerate. There was no reason to suppose that Marcia had had any hand in Cosmo Gallion's death, for Louis assured them that he was a complete stranger to her; she had met him yesterday for the first time. The fact that she must have been just behind him on the stairs when he fell was responsible for her present collapse. She had suffered a great shock. Richard further told the police that Marcia's heart condition was by no means satisfactory, information which stunned Louis, who after the police had left asked, 'Was that the truth—about her heart, I mean?'

'Yes, I'm sorry to say it is . . . she's a sick girl and will need a lot of care. Toni tells me that she underwent several operations after an accident less than a year ago, and I should say they have undermined her constitution to some extent.'

'I had no idea,' Louis was white-faced. 'I knew about the operations, but I understood that Marcia had been given a clean bill of health afterwards.'

'She probably had, but from the cursory examination I

have made, I should say she has never been robust. For one thing—apart from the heart condition—she is very much underweight. She must stay in bed and rest as much as possible.'

Louis was silent for a minute and then he said, 'I know little enough about medicine, but surely the mind must often react upon the body—and Marcia undoubtedly has something on her mind. She said some very odd things when I found her this afternoon. She seems to suffer from a delusion . . . something to do with someone called Monica. She talks of this person in her sleep sometimes, and today after Gallion's accident, before she collapsed, she spoke of her again. It was all more or less incoherent, but she suggested that this Monica was responsible for Gallion's death.'

Richard was silent, but he looked troubled, and Louis went on, 'It must have been the shock . . . she was distraught and didn't know what she was saying.'

'Here's an odd thing,' Richard said. 'Gallion said a word or two before he died—it was when you were speaking to your mother. This is what he said, "The dark girl pushed me . . . she hated me, but I've never seen her before".'

'What on earth could he have meant?'

'There may be some link between his words and what your wife said.'

'How could there be? They were by themselves.'

Richard walked over to the bed and looked down upon Marcia. Her face was very white and childish. Her corn-coloured hair was spread out on the pillow.

'At least,' said Richard, 'Gallion's dying words prove that your wife had nothing to do with the accident. Nobody could describe her as anything but fair.'

'Of course she had nothing to do with it . . . it was an accident . . . a trick of light or something of the kind.'

The door opened and Alma came in. She asked, 'How is she? Is there anything I can do?'

'Nothing at all, Mrs Walters,' Richard said. 'Except to see that she is not disturbed, and when she wakes you could give her some light food. Soup or beaten-up egg. You know where to find me if you want me, unless you would prefer to call in your own doctor.'

'Dr Price is away,' Alma said, 'and surely it would be very unwise to bring an outsider into this. I had better tell you that I overheard what you said just now about Cosmo Gallion's dying words. He said what was true, for I saw her too, she was leaning over the top rail of the staircase, and she was laughing.'

Louis stared at her incredulously. He said, 'But Mother, you couldn't have done—I was there—I saw nobody.'

'Nobody saw her but myself—Louis, don't scoff at this, don't say I imagined it, for she was as clear to me as you and Dr Carlyn are now. But she didn't exist in this world, she was someone I saw out of Time, and I have seen her before. You remember the day you came home with Marcia, I saw her then; she was in the carriage as horribly evil and triumphant as she was today. I was terrified and I fainted.'

'But—it's madness,' Louis gasped. 'You say you saw a spirit. Do you mean to tell me that Cosmo Gallion also saw one? And if so, could a spirit kill?'

'All I know,' Alma said, 'is that the girl, whoever she was, was evil in life and she is still evil—she was capable of murder.'

'Oh, no, that's not true . . . !'

All three turned swiftly towards the bed. Marcia was sitting upright, a brilliant colour in her cheeks, her eyes were bright.

'Monica wasn't wicked—she isn't . . . or if she is, she doesn't know it . . . it's the way she always was. She loved me, she still loves me. But she can't give me up to anyone else, and I can't make her understand that she must. Today she wanted to save me, and so she killed that man. There was no other way.'

Richard went to the bed, he put his hand on Marcia's wrist, and as he did so she fell back on the pillow, and her eyes closed.

'Who is Monica?' Louis asked.

Richard looked at him warningly. He said, 'Don't question her. She's not properly awake . . . she'll be asleep again in a minute.'

But Marcia answered drowsily, 'She was my sister. I was afraid to tell you . . .'

'But my darling, why?' Louis urged. 'How could you be afraid of me?'

Marcia did not seem to hear him. She turned, pressing her face into the pillow. Richard, with his hand still on her wrist, said, 'She's very weak. When she comes out of this sleep don't let her talk. If Toni were not so necessary to her father, she could have spent a few days here to look after her.'

'I can look after her,' Alma said.

There was a deep pity and a strange understanding in her voice. Richard looked at her and was reassured. 'You're fond of her?' he said.

'In my heart I always have been, but I was frightened of her, of something in her which I knew was abnormal. Now I begin to understand and I know it's through no fault of hers that she is sometimes possessed.'

'Possessed!' echoed Louis.

'I can't describe it by any other word, my dear.'

Louis cried out in uncontrollable irritation, 'Oh, for God's sake, don't hand me out that medieval rubbish. Marcia is unbalanced I admit—she has said some odd things, but she has had a bad shock, she has been heavily drugged. What if she is haunted by the memory of a sister she could never tell me about? There is probably some perfectly simple explanation.'

Alma said quietly, 'This sister must have been a peculiar person. Evidently she is dead. But she appears to have been a curse to Marcia in life, and a greater curse since. I can believe, if you cannot, that sometimes a person doesn't wholly die.'

Louis looked at her in stupefaction. He said violently. 'I've never heard such ridiculous rubbish. You've picked on the ravings of a drugged girl and fastened on to them this mad theory.'

'What does Dr Carlyn think?' Alma asked.

Richard, whose face was very grave, said quietly, 'I don't know for certain . . . but to an extent I agree with you. Temporarily at all events your daughter-in-law's mind is deranged, and there is some cause for that derangement . . .'

'She's as sane as you or I,' Alma interrupted vehemently. 'The drug may have loosened her tongue, but what she said was the truth. Remember I have twice seen this Monica looking as alive as any of us here, and also I have seen a painting of her. It was one of Marcia's paintings, and I recognized it. Dr Carlyn, you are a Catholic and your Church does not deny that spirits have the power of materializing. That is why Catholicism forbids any tampering with spiritualism.'

'We do not believe that a soul which departs this world in a state of grace can be called back to it,' Richard said.

'I'm not suggesting that the spirit I saw did die in a state of grace. It's plain to me that when she was on earth this girl, Monica, was a naturally evil person, possessive, dominating, completely unscrupulous. Such a being might well remain on earth to torment her sister, though she was not called back by Marcia, who only longed to be rid of her.'

Richard shook his head. 'You've given us a very strange solution of a mystery, Mrs Walters, and whether it's the right one I cannot judge. But one thing is certain—this girl is in mental distress, and we can pray for her.'

Alma said steadily, 'We can indeed. I know from my own experience that prayers can accomplish miracles, and I shall ask that Marcia be freed from this . . . this horrible entanglement.'

Louis made an impatient movement, and Richard pitied him. It was all very well for Alma, who had arrived at her version of the truth, but to Louis her supernatural explanation was fantastic and ridiculous, and therefore irritating.

However, the immediate good was that Alma had taken Marcia to her heart, that she pitied her and loved her and was prepared to look after her. Richard told himself that all else might well be put aside for the time being.

8

The inquest on Cosmo Gallion was duly held and adjourned for a week in order that Marcia could give her evidence. During the week she had seen scarcely anyone but Alma, though Toni had called on her twice, and Richard had attended her as a doctor.

At Louis's urgent insistence, Richard agreed to prolong his holiday for another week, to the great pleasure of Everard Benham. Toni was also pleased and one day, when she was alone with Richard, said that, if it had not been for this holiday, she doubted if they would ever have come to know each other intimately: as for Alma and Louis, it was the greatest relief to them that they were not obliged to call in the locum who was doing duty for their regular doctor.

'Will Marcia be fit to give her evidence on Tuesday?' she asked.

'Yes, I think so. Mrs Walters is an admirable nurse, she has looked after her devotedly, and has coached her for her examination at the inquest.'

'But should Marcia need coaching? She has only to tell the truth.'

Richard replied after a careful pause, 'There are some truths which cannot be uttered, because they would never be believed.'

Toni said decisively, 'You may be angry with me for saying so, but I feel you are taking a wrong line. I had a long talk with Louis yesterday. It seems you told him to see as little of Marcia as possible; only to pay her a duty visit once or twice a day, but to make them as brief as possible, and to discourage any agitating talk. But if she has some secret trouble, wouldn't it be better for her to tell him about it?'

'At the moment, no,' Richard said. 'Her heart is in a bad way. It can never be strong, and the shock of Gallion's death was great. I don't want her to be further agitated until the strain of the inquest is over.'

'Can't your medical opinion save her from that?' Toni asked.

'Unfortunately, no. We have to face the fact that some suspicion is attached to Marcia. Gallion's death could have been caused by her.'

'But there's no earthly reason why she should have wanted to kill him. They hardly knew each other.'

'Some people might surmise that Gallion was so attracted to her that he tried to seduce her, with the result that in panic she killed him.'

'But that's nonsense too. For one thing Cosmo Gallion was old enough to be Marcia's father, and if he had tried to make love to her, she could have screamed for help, and the others would have heard her. They did hear her scream after he had fallen.'

'No doubt if the question is raised, that fact will be pointed out to the Coroner,' Richard agreed. 'But there's an unpleasant mystery about the accident. Perhaps Louis has told you.'

'Indeed he has. The poor thing is nearly distracted. Marcia has always been rather a mystery to him, but at first she was an enchanting mystery. That didn't last . . .'

'No?'

'No. They've been married three months and Marcia hasn't attempted to fit in with his life—perhaps she can't. I'm fond of her, but from the first I realized, too, there was something fey about her. Alma realized it too, and accepted it, but it upsets Louis. He has never understood her. She loves solitude, she takes no interest in worldly matters, she cares nothing for money—as you know, she's willing to give up the bulk of her inheritance to start this convalescent home . . .'

'Does he want her to care about money?' Richard asked.

'No—but he wants her to be ordinary . . . or at least more akin to the average woman.'

'Isn't it odd,' said Richard, 'that a man will fall in love

with the very qualities which afterwards rasp him? Marcia must always have been unlike other people; for that reason she charmed Louis, but now he would prefer to have her standardized.'

'He probably thought she had the ordinary qualities as well,' Toni said. 'Louis needs peace and a sense of security in order to do good work. Marcia can give him neither. Alma's theory is that she is possessed by the spirit of a dead sister of whom Louis had never heard when he married her. He doesn't believe this, of course. To him it's a dangerous and neurotic delusion.'

'Do you think it's a delusion, Toni?'

'I don't know . . . I had a curious sensation once when I was with Marcia . . . I thought there was someone in the room with us, someone evil, but I dare say I was wrought up and nervous, and could have imagined anything.' And then, as he was silent, she asked, 'Do you believe in this possession fantasy?'

'I've never been more uncertain of what is fantasy or what is reality. I only know that Marcia needs help, and that I am incapable of helping her. She is wandering blindly in a world of her own.'

Toni sighed deeply. 'It's a ghastly tangle. Most people would say that Marcia is mad, and let it go at that.'

'Then Mrs Walters is also mad. Remember she saw this dark girl, remember too that Gallion spoke of her—they were his last words.'

'It's all so horrible,' Toni cried. 'Why should this thing have happened to Louis and his mother? They were happy, Louis had his work . . . his ambition . . .'

'And he had you, Toni, before he met Marcia Norman.'

She looked at him with startled eyes. 'How did you know?'

'Through a combination of trivialities. Mrs Walters remarked once that you and Louis had been the greatest of friends since your return from America; Louis himself said you were the finest girl he knew; all of you have at one time or another suggested that his love for his wife was a sudden, blinding infatuation, and that his marriage was too hastily entered upon. You are in his confidence, he comes to you with his troubles, probably tells you that already his married life is a disappointment to him.'

'But I only want Marcia to be happy, and to make Louis happy,' Toni said with trembling lips. 'I'm doing her no harm. I *ask* nothing for myself.'

'Do you not? It seems to me that you also asked for peace and security. When you spoke of marrying me as though it might be a possibility, were you not thinking that such a marriage might help you to forget Louis? You suggested working with me in my dispensary, not for the love of it, but because you hoped to lose yourself in such work and sublimate your unhappiness.'

'Was that wrong?' asked Toni, her voice hurt and shaking. 'If I love him, isn't it natural that I should try to think of some way in which I can put him out of my mind? As for marrying you, I always knew and so did you that that could never happen unless I loved you sufficiently to accept your creed, and give you all my heart.'

'I'm not blaming you,' Richard said. 'I understand, but that doesn't make it the less bitter.'

She sighed. 'It's all in the past. I told you that before. I did think once that Louis cared, but then he met Marcia. He never asked me to marry him, he doesn't know I loved him, and it's all over anyway.'

'Over, while you live within a mile of his home, while he comes to you for sympathy, while you are in and out of his house nearly every day?'

Now, at his tone, her anger was aroused, and she said, 'Surely you don't imagine I am carrying on a love affair with him?'

'No—but I think his heart has turned from his wife, I think he now realizes you were the woman he should have married, and that he deeply regrets his mistake. Be honest with yourself, don't you think and hope that this is so?'

'Of course I don't. It's only because of Father that I stay here at all. Besides, lately I've changed—I'm fond of Louis, but I'm no more than fond. I want him to be happy with Marcia, which must mean I've stopped loving in a possessive way.'

'People can stop being possessive when they know that

that way there is no hope for them. There are more subtle means of getting what you want.'

'What means?'

'It must be obvious to you that through your sympathy and understanding you can now become indispensable to Louis Walters. You have established a new bond with him.'

'Well, what if I have?' she cried defiantly. 'Doesn't he need sympathy and understanding, and who else can give it to him? Marcia is ill, Alma is absorbed in her—I am the only one who wants to help him.'

'He should be strong enough to stand alone, and to sort things out for himself,' Richard said, with what Toni considered an inhuman austerity.

'But few people are as strong as that,' she protested. 'You're jealous, Richard, and you can't be fair to either of us.'

'I dare say that's quite true,' he said, and looked so dejected that pity swept Toni in a sudden flood. She wanted to comfort him and could not, for how can the uncertain heart comfort? She knew herself so little, could not have said at this moment if Louis meant more to her than Richard. She only knew that she suffered to see him suffer, which in itself was a little act of love.

'I'm sorry, my dear,' she said, and looking up at her, he saw that she was indeed sorry.

'Everything will find its own level,' he said. 'I don't want to be unfair to you, but it's difficult to be here, and I wish now that I hadn't agreed to stay on for a further week. The Walterses are wrong in thinking they can't do without me, and in London there is much work waiting for me.'

'I believe in the end you will be glad you stayed,' Toni answered. 'By the time you go this problem may be solved. I have an odd feeling that everything is moving towards a climax of some sort—though whether it is one we shall welcome remains to be seen.'

At the adjourned inquest which Marcia attended, she behaved perfectly. She looked pale but composed, and so young that this in itself was an asset to her. She wore a white woollen dress under her dark fur coat, for it was a chilly day, and a small white hat which resembled a bonnet.

Clearly and with little emotion she related what had occurred immediately before Cosmo Gallion fell to his death. They had been talking about ordinary things, she said, actually about her scheme for turning The Red Towers into a home for convalescents. He had been interested in her plans. They had mounted the stairs to the turret for the sake of the view, and had stayed there talking. Gallion had been the first to leave the turret room. She had been lingering at the window, when she heard the sound of his fall and his cry as he hurtled down the winding staircase. She had screamed herself then, but she had been paralysed, unable to move, and hadn't known that Gallion was dead, until later. It had been a dreadful shock, and since then she had been ill.

The Coroner treated Marcia considerately, and was evidently impressed with the clearness and candour of her evidence. He asked her few questions and it was a foregone conclusion that the verdict would be one of accidental death.

Louis had expected nothing else, but Alma had had her doubts, and she watched Marcia intently as she gave evidence. It was a tremendous relief that she acquitted herself so well. As they all walked out of the court-room together, Alma pressed the girl's arm and said, 'You were wonderful. Now you have only to forget about it all. The papers made headlines of the accident for a day or two, but after tomorrow, when the inquest will be reported, there will be no more of it.'

Toni said compassionately, 'Nobody seems to have cared about Cosmo Gallion. He must have been a very lonely man, knowing quantities of people, but with no real friend.'

'If a person lives and dies that way, it must be because he deserves it,' Marcia said in a hard and bitter voice.

Alma looked as much frightened as surprised, and when Louis suggested they should lunch at the local hotel, she said quickly, 'I think it would be better if we were to go straight home. Marcia is tired with her ordeal, and Dr Carlyn and Toni will join us, I hope. I planned lunch before I left this morning.'

Everyone during the meal talked volubly, with the exception of Marcia, but as she was usually silent, this did not seem unnatural. By mutual consent, talk of the inquest was avoided. Richard was drawn out to speak of his experiences in his East End practice, but he only touched on the lighter side of this. There was plenty of humour in the poor quarters, even if there was also plenty of tragedy.

It was not until the end of lunch, when they were lingering over their coffee, that Marcia spoke, and then she electrified them all. She rose from her seat, and stood with both hands resting lightly on the table, by her attitude calling for silence and attention. It was, thought Toni, almost as though she was intending to make a speech.

'Please,' she said. 'I have something to say, and I am glad you are all here together. Dr Carlyn has not allowed me to speak before, because he was worried about my health and thought I might be really ill if further agitated, but I have to risk that now. I can't be silent any longer. I must tell you my story, and I want all four of you to hear it, because with the exception of Dr Carlyn you are bound up in my life. He is almost a stranger to me, though I did hope at one time that he would be my friend. Because he is a doctor, and because he is a religious person who believes in doing good for its own sake, I thought he might be able to show me how to free myself. But I never had the chance to find out if he could help me, because my fear was diverted. I had something else to think about.'

'Marcia . . . dear . . .' Alma broke in.

Marcia turned to look at her, a grave, affectionate look. 'You understand something, Alma, and you've been good to me, but you don't understand about Cosmo Gallion. You don't know who he was, or why Monica wanted to kill him. I can't blame her for that. She could see no other way out, and though she's jealous of me because I'm still alive, and because I can do without her, she loves me terribly, and she won't let anyone hurt me, if she can help it. Cosmo Gallion wanted to hurt me.'

Louis bent across the table to her. He said earnestly, 'My dearest, that's a delusion. You are not well, Marcia, your mind is upset. Give yourself time, and you will come back to yourself. Dr Carlyn will tell you that what I say is true.'

'Will you, Dr Carlyn?' Marcia asked.

Across the table their eyes met, and Richard, after a moment, said: 'No, you had better speak now, and we had better listen. I have to safeguard your physical health, but I knew the time would come when you would insist on a hearing.'

'It won't make me ill to speak,' Marcia said. 'It will be a relief to me. Afterwards I will rest; I will do everything you tell me I ought to do.'

'That's a bargain,' Richard said, and he smiled at her, his professional, medical smile.

'I'll have to go back over twenty years,' Marcia said. 'My mother was very unhappy before I was born. She was a Catholic, and she gave up her Faith. I don't know why. I've heard that she turned from it in hatred. I know very little about her, she never spoke to me about religious matters, she belonged to no Church at the time I knew her. She was quite young when she married my father, but the marriage was unhappy from the first; my father never really loved her, and they quarrelled—especially about money. My mother was wealthy, and he was clever . . . I don't think he had anything but what he made by his work as a journalist. He left her before we were born, though it's unlikely he intended the separation to be permanent—her money must have been too important to him—but from that time my mother believed the marriage was cursed, because she had turned away from her religion, and when we were born she was sure of it. You see we were twins—and not just ordinary twins. We were joined together.'

Marcia paused and looked round the table. Her gaze rested longest upon Louis, and he half rose in his chair.

'How do you mean . . . joined together?'

'You've heard of such cases, Louis. You must have heard of them,' Marcia said. 'Such twins are called Siamese. I didn't know that until a little while ago, when I read of a similar case in a book I found in the library. The name has come down from two Chinese boys who were born joined together. They lived in Siam at the beginning of the last century. Monica and I were joined together—our shoulders and our sides . . . my left side was joined to her right side, but her heart was on her right side. It was so close to mine, that we almost shared the same heart-beats. Have you heard of such a case, Dr Carlyn?'

Richard, inured to shocks, was yet regarding her with the deepest pity and concern. Although she seemed calm, he realized that she was strung up to the highest pitch of nervous intensity. She was revealing her secret because it had become unendurable to conceal it any longer, but in doing so she was putting her fate to the test, and also putting Louis's love for her to the test.

'Certainly I have heard of similar cases,' Richard said, 'though none has come my way. How such twins are joined varies, and I can't say off-hand if any others have been connected in the way you describe.'

'We led a strange life, Monica and I,' Marcia went on, 'but we were used to it, and didn't know how strange it was. My mother looked upon us as the symbol of a sin, which she believed could never be forgiven. I don't think she tried to get forgiveness, for she never went outside our house and grounds, and no priest ever came to see her. Sometimes we saw a doctor, the one who brought us into the world, for I wasn't strong, though Monica was. But he died two or three years ago, and after that we saw no one. My father came to see my mother once, after we were born, but he was horrified and revolted, and didn't come again. They parted then for ever.

'Monica and I were not alike. She was shorter than I and she was dark; she had a sallow complexion and black curly hair. I was always very fair. Neither were we alike in our natures. Our—disability wasn't so hard for me as for Monica, because she wanted to do all sorts of active things like climbing trees and swimming and she loved to walk . . . oh, how she walked, for miles and miles round the grounds, and of course I had to walk too, though I was often exhausted, and the doctor forbade it. Janet forbade it too, and she would see it didn't happen. She loved me, but Monica didn't care for her, and Janet could do nothing with her. She didn't want to learn, but I loved it. It was difficult to teach Monica even to read or write, but I found all my pleasure in reading. That made Monica angry and jealous, because she wanted to share everything with me, but this she couldn't share. She used to insist that we were really one person, but I knew we were two people, even though we could never be apart. She would snatch a book from my hand, and she often tried to tear my books up. She was jealous of everything I liked; once she killed a kitten I loved, she strangled it, and after that I would never have another pet. She loved only me, but it was chiefly because she insisted I was part of her . . . oh, you don't know, none of you knows the bondage it was . . . for I wasn't like her . . . I wasn't.'

She broke off, and across the table Alma stretched out her hand to her. 'Marcia darling, haven't you told us enough?' she said.

Marcia looked at Alma's hand lying on the table so near to her, and for an instant her hand touched it. 'I must finish now,' she said. 'This isn't such a shock and surprise to you, Alma, as it is to Louis, for you have guessed something these last days. I deceived Louis when I married him; I couldn't tell him the truth. We were in love and I was terrified that he wouldn't love me any more; besides, Janet told me never to tell anyone, and I obeyed her. She had been my ally against Monica, though that sounds dreadful, for we were sisters, and I did love her, though not as she loved me. Oh, Louis, please forgive me for what I did to you.'

There was a moment's silence before Louis found his voice, and then he said, 'There's nothing for me to forgive . . . I asked no questions. I loved you.'

'But would you have loved me, if you had known my story? Cosmo Gallion was sure that you wouldn't, that you couldn't. He said you would be disgusted.'

'But what on earth has Cosmo Gallion to do with it?' Toni asked, speaking for the first time.

Marcia brushed her hand across her eyes, as though in weary bewilderment. She said, 'I'm not telling this the right way . . . I meant to make it like a story, starting from the beginning and getting right down to today. Meeting Cosmo Gallion, and finding out who he was, is almost the end of the story. He recognized me when he saw me the other day; it seems I am like my mother, and he was the man who married her and left her, and was my father. Of course he could not imagine what had happened, for the last time he saw me was when I was a baby, and he saw Monica too. He was a vile man. He blackmailed me. He told me he would be silent if I gave him a great deal of money. I was afraid for him to tell Louis, but it wasn't only that, he said he would publish it all in the papers, so that everyone would know . . . all about how Monica and I had been born, and how the operation was successful which gave me, as the surgeon and doctors said, a separate life.'

'So there was a motive,' Louis said harshly. 'You did have reason to kill Gallion.'

He stared at Marcia as though for the first time he was really trying to comprehend her, to assess her. But she did not flinch from his look, but gazed at him entreatingly, with humility.

'Yes, I had a motive, but it didn't occur to me to kill him. That was Monica's doing. Oh Louis, if you could only believe me, if you could only realize how hard I've tried to be myself, but she wouldn't leave me. Over and over again she has raged about the operation; has said that I should have died when she died.'

'Oh, heaven!' cried Louis. 'Now it's the old delusion once again.'

His voice was hard and impatient. He got up from the table and flung himself down on the settee in the window alcove. All the patience which he had shown during the last week had come to an end, and his anxiety found expression in a violent irritation.

'It isn't a delusion, Louis, how I wish it were . . . ask your mother if it is.'

'I've no intention of asking anyone. If my mother wishes to believe in this nonsense, then she must. I'm only thankful you behaved sanely at the Coroner's court, otherwise you might have been under arrest by now.'

'You can't really think I killed Cosmo Gallion!' Marcia cried. 'I didn't—I didn't. I know it was wrong to deceive you, I know you may never love me again, but it's true about Monica. She was part of me, and she has never left me. After the accident, when our three bodies were discovered, I alone was breathing, and Janet arranged for me to be . . . be given a chance. A famous surgeon took up the challenge. Somehow or other he kept me going by drugs or injections—I'm vague about that, for I don't remember any of it, and then he performed the operation. I was severed from Monica who was dead.'

'It was an iniquitous thing to do!' Louis cried.

They all stared at him, Toni and Alma in horror, Marcia with tears of bitter pain. It was Richard who said quietly, 'Iniquitous to save her life?'

Louis suddenly seemed to come to himself. With a violent effort he resumed his usual reasonable manner. 'No, of course I don't mean that,' he said. 'But—it was a ghastly risk, he might have killed her.'

Only to Marcia did his explanatory words carry conviction. It was obvious to the others that he had meant something very different, but she seized upon them eagerly. 'Oh, but darling, think! There was no alternative. How could I live joined to someone who was dead? The operation was a triumph. Later there were minor operations, but they were successful too . . . there's only the faintest, smallest scar. I was happy, I thought I could start again; the doctors told me I could, and so did Janet. It was so exciting those first few weeks . . . I thought it was only imagination that from time to time I felt Monica close to me. But after we were married I knew it wasn't imagination, for she was terribly jealous of you, Louis, and she got stronger and stronger. She wanted me to be happy with her, but not with someone else. She talked to me and I had to talk back—she was with me in my dreams and sometimes when I was awake. Once or twice I thought I saw her, but I was never sure of that until she killed—our father. She was furious with him for threatening me. I heard her say clearly, "Nobody shall hurt you," and then I saw her. She was there in the turret room, she was part of me, and then she was not me any longer but her own self, standing there beside me, and laughing because he thought he could make me do as he wished. She followed him out of the turret room, and I knew what she would do, but I couldn't help it . . . I couldn't move. She came up behind him and she was like a cloud covering him. He hadn't a chance—he couldn't prevail against her because she had her own power . . . I saw him go crashing down the stairs, and then Monica laughed . . .'

She broke off, her voice shaking on the last words, and Alma said, 'It's true . . . I told you, Louis, that I saw her too. She was standing there, leaning over the rail and laughing.'

'Oh, God!' Louis cried. 'Surely everything is bad enough without this mischievous nonsense! Mother, how on earth can you support such a mad story?'

'It's fortunate for you,' said Alma, 'that I can honestly support it. I am the only person who can prove that your wife is innocent.'

In the silence which followed Marcia abruptly sat down, and folding her arms on the table, dropped her head down upon them. Richard went over to Louis and spoke to him in a low voice.

'Go to her, say something to her, and then she must be put to bed and given a sedative.'

Slowly and reluctantly Louis approached Marcia. He put his hand on her shoulder and said gently, 'Don't worry any more. It is all over now, and you can forget about it.'

Marcia raised her face and looked up at him; there were tears in her eyes and her lips were trembling. 'Does it make any difference to you?' she asked.

'No—why should it?'

He stooped and lightly kissed her cheek, passing his hand over her fair hair. It was not, thought Toni watching him, too obviously a lie. For one who was no actor, it was a commendable performance.

'So much now depends on Louis,' Alma said.

'But I thought he behaved very well,' Toni said. 'It was

a horrible shock to him—it must have been. It shocked me.'

'Yes, of course it was a shock, and he wouldn't have reacted to it so well if Dr Carlyn hadn't been there. That's a fine young man, Toni, and he has been more than good to us throughout this trouble.'

'It's his nature to be good to people,' said Toni.

'Yes, I believe it is. My dear, he is a far kinder and better person than my poor Louis.'

There was a personal touch about this remark which was unwelcome to Toni. She wished Alma were less clear-sighted. It seemed as though she invariably saw further than other people. She had known that Toni was in love with Louis, and now she evidently suspected that Richard was in love with her.

'You ought not to think hardly of Louis,' she said repressively. 'Richard is a doctor and is trained to withstand shocks—besides, Marcia's story didn't affect him personally as it affected Louis. It was a terribly unpleasant thing for him to have to hear.'

'To my mind,' Alma said, 'the thing which should have most upset him was that Marcia kept all this from him. It shows she had little confidence in him. The—the malformation, call it what you will, was no fault of hers, and since the operation was performed successfully there was no need to dwell on it. But the fact that her twin sister has never really died is alarming.'

'Alma,' cried Toni wildly, 'don't talk in such a way—about her twin. I can't bear it—it's all ghastly.'

'But darling,' Alma soothed, 'I'm not suggesting it's hopeless. If Louis acts properly, there can be happiness for them both. He must convince Marcia he loves her beyond everything, that his love is stronger than any evil, supernatural spell, and then when he has convinced her of this, there are various methods which can be tried, such as exorcism, treatment by a doctor and hypnotism, though it's the first in which I put my faith. Toni, she is well worth saving.'

'You love her very much, don't you?'

'Yes—now I do, I love her completely. I was afraid of

her, but that was when I was groping in the dark, knowing there was some mystery, but not understanding what it was. But these last few days I've learnt to admire Marcia. I've seen her struggling to free herself. I've seen her succeed and become completely exhausted; I've seen her vanquished, but she has fought all she could. Now, though she is under a dreadful curse, I'm concerned as to whether my son is good enough for her, for I know that she, the real Marcia, is good enough for any man.'

'She's fortunate to have you,' Toni said. 'Oh dear, even now I can't altogether believe that this dead girl has any power over her. I'm sure Marcia believes it though, and if it's a trouble of the mind a doctor may be able to help her.'

'My faith is in exorcism. Even in these days it's conceivable that a holy person has the power to cast out devils. Marcia practises no religion, but it appears that Janet Cameron told her that when she and Monica were infants and not expected to live, they were baptized by a Catholic priest, therefore she does belong to that Church. I wondered if I could get help for her. There's Father Arnon in Seacrest, and I know him slightly. I might ask him, though he's not the sort of person I should choose. He's old and feeble and not a very clever person.'

Toni said decisively, 'I don't think you should do anything without consulting Louis. It wouldn't be fair to him and he would resent it.'

'I suppose he would. Very well then, I'll speak to him tomorrow. We have all gone through enough for today. Thank heaven Marcia is asleep and at peace for the time being. Louis has gone off for a long walk; he said he had to be alone.'

'And you look worn out. Go to bed yourself. Tell Hetty to bring tea and toast up to your room, and leave something cold for Louis so that he can have it when he comes in. I expect he will be relieved not to have to talk to you or to anyone until tomorrow. I must get home—I've been too long away and Richard is keeping Father company.'

'We're all very selfish to you, dear Toni, we've absorbed you into our family and it isn't fair. Please thank Dr

Carlyn for me. I'm so grateful to him and he said he would too long away and Richard is keeping Father company.'

Toni left with a sense of relief, and with a sense of gratitude that Richard would be at home to meet her. She had had as much as she could endure, and for the first time in her life was glad to turn her back upon Meadow House.

9

The ringing of a distant bell roused Toni as she was dropping off to sleep. She realized that it was the telephone, still a novelty and an unusual asset in a private house. Theirs had been installed when her father had become seriously ill, but incoming calls were rare. Toni unwillingly got out of bed and went down the stairs to answer this one. It was past eleven, and as Stella was at a party, the rest of the household had gone to bed at a reasonable hour. Toni was too sleepy to wonder who could be telephoning her, but she was startled into alert attention when she heard Louis's voice.

'Toni, are you alone?' he asked.

'Yes—the others have gone to bed. What is wrong?' she asked anxiously, and heard his bitter, ironical laugh.

'Pretty well everything, I should think. I can't sleep at this hour and I was longing to hear your voice.'

'How is Marcia?' Toni asked. 'Richard hoped she would have a long sleep.'

'So she will, she's been very efficiently doped—I wish I had. Look here, Toni, I must see you. At the moment you seem to be the only sane person in the world. Here, with my mother and Marcia it's like being shut up in a lunatic asylum. Oh God, what a fool I've been!'

'But what has happened since I saw you?' Toni asked in alarm.

'Oh, nothing, I suppose, except that I've had time to

assess everything and to realize how hopeless it all is. I've made the most ghastly mistake and somehow or other I must put things right. I can't go on like this. Toni, you know the fool I've been. What I told you before I left for Spain still stands. It's as though I've been dragged into a bog and am only just starting to pull myself out of it.'

'You mustn't talk like that,' she protested.

'I agree it isn't the wisest thing to do over the telephone. But surely I can see you tomorrow. I need your advice and your help. This is an S O S.'

'Of course you can see me,' Toni said. 'Why not come over here?'

'I hoped you would suggest it. I know Carlyn will be seeing Marcia tomorrow; he said he would be here around eleven o'clock. There's no need for me to be here, so I'll drive over if you will stay in for me.'

'I will. Try and get some sleep, Louis. I know you have all had a succession of shocks, but the worst is over now. Good night, my dear.'

She hung up before he could reply and went back to bed, but not to sleep for a long while. She realized that now indeed she had a problem on her hands, but she thought she could tackle it. Louis, weary and bewildered, was in the mood to believe that his marriage was a complete failure; he was even thinking sentimentally of herself, which was disconcerting, but Toni was certain that she could soon make him see reason. He had never loved her, though to an extent she represented consolation and peace, and never more so than at this minute. But it was Marcia who needed him.

It would be quite a good idea, mused Toni, for Louis to take her away for a time, and certainly she should have first-rate medical advice. Toni ruled out the suggestion of exorcism; that was the kind of mystical thing which the mystical Alma might be expected to suggest. A specialist in mental illness was the person to deal with Marcia's obsession.

Eventually she fell asleep, but throughout the night she dreamed unhappily of Marcia—saw her crying out for help, and knew most miserably that she was powerless to aid her in any way.

When Louis called the next morning, Toni was glad that Richard had already departed for Meadow House. Stella had been driving into Seacrest and, prompted by Toni, she had offered Richard a lift. He would probably be away for a couple of hours, for it was more than likely that Alma would ask him to stay for lunch in order to discuss Marcia's state of health with him.

Everard Benham, who was not so well that morning, was keeping to his bed. It seemed too great an effort for him to be dressed and helped into his wheel chair and as it was a chilly morning he could not have stayed for long in the garden.

Toni saw him comfortably settled with a book and the daily papers. She went down to the room which had once been his study and put a match to the fire which was already laid.

She was kneeling on the rug watching the sticks and paper kindle when Louis was shown in, and then she got to her feet to greet him. His appearance surprised and shocked her. In the course of twenty-four hours his face had become haggard, and his eyes were sunken. Toni took his hand and urged him into the big winged chair which had once been her father's favourite.

'I know it's early,' she said, but we're both going to have a glass of sherry before you say a word. Nobody will interrupt us, and there's no hurry, so take your time. I'm sorry you're miserable, Louis, and I do understand. If Marcia had told you before you married her, everything would have been different.'

'Yes, very different,' Louis said grimly, 'for I shouldn't have married her.'

'But why should it make such a difference? It was an accident of birth . . . Marcia wasn't responsible.'

'Nor is a cretin or any freak responsible for their abnormalities. None the less they are repulsive, poor creatures.'

'You can't compare Marcia to a freak. She's not only beautiful, but good and intelligent.'

There was silence for a moment, while Louis drained his

glass, and Toni replenished it. Then he said, 'I know it's unfair to her—but she fills me with horror.'

'Louis!'

'You can't blame me for a nerve reaction. I'm finished, I can never live with her. To me she's abnormal, horrible. I tried to behave decently yesterday, not to show what I felt, but I can't do it again. For nothing in this world could I ever kiss her, much less sleep with her . . .'

He broke off with a gesture which was more eloquent than words, for it was one of repudiation, final and complete. Toni said, her voice warm with compassion, 'But the poor little thing . . . you can't just discard her—she's your wife. If this dead girl Monica had been her ordinary twin, you wouldn't have thought anything of it.'

'They weren't ordinary twins,' he said curtly.

'But it's not so very different.'

'You only say that because you haven't thought about it . . . as I've been forced to think of it. God knows, I tried not to, but since she told me I've done nothing but visualize their closeness—and what it entailed. Such intimacy was disgusting, indecent.'

'Oh, how can you!' Toni cried in anger.

'One can't control one's thoughts, Toni, and mine I admit have been obscene. Remember they were never separated . . . couldn't be. They were to all intents and purposes one person, and now I feel that I was married not only to Marcia, but to that dead girl . . . I feel as though I mated with something decayed and corrupt. Don't look at me like that, as though I'm out of my mind.'

'But it sounds almost as though you are,' she said slowly.

'I'm sorry, but mad or sane I can't go on. Use your imagination, and try to realize my feelings. Every time I took Marcia in my arms, I should think of that other. Remember that until the first operation was performed, she was fastened to a dead girl, united to corruption. To me it's as though she isn't a whole person, as though when her twin died she became incomplete.'

'I think you're reacting to this in a shockingly morbid way,' said Toni severely. 'You heard Marcia say that she and her twin were absolutely different in appearance and disposition.'

'Yes, and you also heard her say or at least infer that Monica was by far the more dominant character. I don't believe in this fantastic story of haunting, but I do believe that Marcia has some kind of a dual personality and that this dates from the time of Monica's death. They were united and they drew from one another, were indivisible; therefore whatever unpleasant characteristics Marcia possesses she derives from her twin.'

'Let's get this straight,' Toni said. 'You deny that the spirit of Monica lives on in the sense that Alma believes, but you do think that Marcia absorbed her personality when she died.'

'Yes, that's what I said. I quite believe she was a sweet, dreamy, lovable girl, and that Monica was a problem child. They divided one character between them. Few if any of us are altogether sweet, altogether noble, nor are we altogether bad, but these two girls apparently were, while they were both alive. Do you see what I am getting at?'

'I do,' Toni said sombrely, 'and I think it's perfectly horrible, worse than Alma's theory, which is supported by the fact that she claims to have twice seen Monica. If one were to carry your theory to its logical conclusion then it was Marcia who killed Cosmo Gallion.'

'I believe it was, but I could get over that, for she had provocation.'

'Marcia could not hurt anyone—I believe her story if you don't.'

'I do believe it up to a point. What happened is that Marcia switched over to Monica. As I say, she has a dual personality. If I continued to live with her, I should be living with two women.'

'That's ridiculous!'

'It doesn't seem ridiculous to me.'

'Marcia's not strong—it will nearly kill her if you leave her,' Toni said.

'People are tougher than you suppose; in any case I've no intention of making a brutal break. Fortunately I had a letter from my publishers this morning, which I was able to show Marcia—she was awake then. They want me up in London for a few days; there's a new contract pending and a literary luncheon at which I'm expected to make a speech. It all fits in very conveniently. Marcia thinks I am only going for a few days, but I shall probably not be back for weeks—that's one reason why I had to see you.'

Toni ignored the last words. She said pitifully, 'Oh, Louis, didn't you ever really love her? You seemed to. A few weeks ago, you were infatuated with her.'

'That's exactly the right word. I was infatuated. It was never real. She was so lovely, and so strange that she bowled me over. For the time being I forgot you, or seemed to forget you, for I know now that it was really you . . . the other was a mirage.'

'I can't listen to this sort of thing.'

'But, my darling, you must—just this once. After today I promise I'll never speak of it again, until I am free.'

'Free!' she echoed.

'I must be free eventually, Toni. While I'm away I shall ask Marcia to divorce me. Needless to say, your name won't be mentioned—I can arrange for some other woman to act as co-respondent.'

'You can't do such a thing to her. She hasn't deserved it.'

'It's not a question of deserving it, though if it comes to that, she did deceive me, and it was because of her deception that the marriage took place. But putting that aside, I can only say it's impossible for me to act as her husband, and therefore for her own sake she ought to be free. She's young enough to start life all over again, perhaps to marry some man who is less squeamish.'

'Poor girl,' Toni said. 'That's the second time she has been told she was free. After the operation the doctors assured her she had been given a fresh start. Louis, she hasn't a friend in the world except your mother and myself. What is to become of her unselfish scheme, what is to happen about The Red Towers?'

'She will have to sell the place, I suppose—she may lose money on it, but that won't be a serious matter to Marcia. As for being lonely, no woman with her looks and her money is likely to be lonely for long. I don't mean that cynically . . . but as she's interested in philanthropy there will be plenty of people only too eager to put her in the right way to spend her money. Your friend Carlyn for one.'

'Yes, I'm sure Richard will try to help her,' Toni said.

Her voice was sad and her eyes, as they rested on Louis, were sadder. It was true, as Alma had once said, though she had spoken with an amused affection, that he was spoilt, that all the world had combined to spoil him, and the results of this spoiling were now to be seen. To some extent Toni could understand his repugnance, his revulsion. Love was not to be forced, and if he had ceased to love Marcia he was not to be blamed, tragedy though it was. But callousness was inexcusable. Her old love for him wrenched at her heart, but she condemned him.

'You seem to have any amount of pity for Marcia, but none at all for me,' Louis said in an injured voice.

'Do you deserve pity?'

'I don't know about deserving it, but no man wants to have his marriage broken up within a few months of his wedding. Toni, try to look at things from my point of view. Oh, darling, you did love me, and not so long ago . . .'

'I never said so.'

'You didn't need to say it. I saw it in your eyes. I knew you would give me the answer when I asked you, and I meant to ask you. I never for a moment supposed I should meet anyone who could come before you, and it was only for a short time that Marcia did come before you.'

The blood rushed to Toni's cheeks, her heart thudded with anger and agitation. She said coldly, 'I could tell you a lie, Louis, but I won't. I *was* in love with you, and I was fool enough to show it, though when you came home with your bride it suited you to behave as though there had never been anything between us. It was easier then for you to persuade yourself I hadn't cared. As far as I can see you always take the easiest way out of a situation. When you wanted Marcia, you couldn't consider me any more than you can consider her now. There's nothing I can do to prevent you from leaving her, from getting a divorce if she will give you one—but count me out of it. And now will you please go . . . we have nothing more to say to one another.'

With her blazing cheeks and her eyes flashing, she had never looked more desirable and Louis said softly, 'I understand you, Toni, and I admire you. I realize that it's useless to plead with you now. You are Marcia's friend, and you will stand by her. That's what I should expect of you. But when she's no longer my wife, then all will be different, and believe me, my darling, I shan't be a fool twice. You can be certain now that there's no other woman in the world for me.'

Protests rose to Toni's lips, but before she could utter them, Louis rose, opened the door and was gone. Toni stood there trembling. But she did not think long of herself; her thoughts went to Marcia in what would soon be her unspeakable desolation, and then suddenly she, who so rarely cried, found that the tears were streaming down her cheeks. She flung herself into the big chair where Louis had been sitting, and violent sobs shook her. It was thus that Richard found her. She did not hear the door open, did not realize that he was there, until he touched her shoulder, and then she looked up, with her face all disfigured, and her lips trembling. Richard sat down on the arm of the chair and took one of her hands in his. He said very gently, 'Louis Walters has been here I suppose. I passed his carriage on the road.'

She nodded and after a moment she found her voice: 'He's talking of leaving Marcia, of getting her to divorce him. I'm terribly unhappy.'

'Unhappy because there's a chance that he may soon be free?'

'I want him to make a success of his marriage, and to make Marcia happy.'

'What about your own happiness, Toni?'

'I shan't find it that way, by trampling on the ruins of another woman's life.'

'No, I don't think you will,' he said gently. 'But I can't see much happiness for Marcia either, unless Louis suffers a change of heart.'

'Oh, if only he could,' Toni said. 'I wish she hadn't told him. Sometimes I think the love of confession is one of the greatest weaknesses to which human beings are subject.'

'It can be,' Richard agreed.

'I do understand how the twin business has affected Louis,' Toni said miserably. 'But if only he could take it differently. I still have hope that when he is away from Marcia, and has time to think it all over, he will come back to her. I'm sure he will do nothing in a hurry.'

'You make sufficient excuses for this chap—do you still love him?' Richard asked, and strove to keep the anger out of his voice.

'I don't know . . . I haven't thought . . . or rather I've thought to no purpose. Didn't I tell you that before? I only know it gives me no pleasure to see him, and I can't bear to think of the blow that is coming to Marcia.'

'As you say,' Richard remarked, 'it's a good thing he is leaving her this afternoon. Marcia sent you a message. She wants you to have tea with her. I've told her she may get up if she takes things quietly.'

Toni said despairingly, 'I know it's cowardly of me, but I wish I needn't see her—I wish I needn't go near Meadow House.'

'But this is not the time to stay away, Toni. Marcia has been through a tremendous crisis. She needs all the friends she has.'

'I know it, and of course I'll go over this afternoon. It's horribly selfish of me to think of myself.'

'You don't strike me as being particularly selfish,' Richard said, and the tenderness he could not control crept into his voice.

Toni put her hand on his and squeezed it. She said, 'I'm so fond of you, but just lately it's as though I'm being tossed around in a maelstrom; I can't sort out my feelings.'

'Never mind, I can wait.'

'You're the best person in the world, Richard.'

He laughed and said, 'I should hate to think it; it would put the rest of humanity in a pretty state if none of them were better than I. Toni dear, perhaps the best virtue I have is that of faithfulness. I do love you very dearly, and

I always shall. It's quite likely you will never be my wife but, if you don't, there will never be another woman for me.'

'When you talk in that way I feel as though I am spoiling your life,' Toni said remorsefully.

'Nothing of the kind; I have my work, and it's a great deal to know you, to be your friend.'

Toni was silent. Her heart was torn. Why couldn't she take this deep love and all the good it would bring to her? She was desperately tired and how often she also felt desperately alone. In England she had few close friends, because during her long stay in America most of them had half forgotten her. The girls with whom she had been at school had married, the boys she had known had gone abroad or to London. It was a narrow restricted circle in which she now lived, for although some of Stella's friends had made a friendly gesture to her, there was no individual who especially appealed to her.

Alma and Louis at Meadow House, and her father at home, had filled her life—but soon her father would leave her, and now Meadow House was not the haven it once had been. She would have to start out in the world again and with little spirit for the uphill path.

Even the work as Richard's dispenser and auxiliary nurse, which had seemed so interesting, did not greatly entice her. She had the yearning which comes upon most women for a home of her own, a man to look after, children to love. But all these good things must be forgone because she could not love enough.

She could be fond of Louis, and make excuses for him; she could just as certainly be fond of Richard and admire him for his fine qualities, but she was too numbed to feel love for either of them. It was as though the events of the last few weeks had stunned her.

'I don't know what to say,' she said. 'I don't know what to do.'

'Do nothing—only be kind to Marcia, don't let her suspect that Louis has changed towards her. I am speaking now as a doctor. That girl is in a precarious condition. Although I have many worse cases waiting for me in

London, I'm loath to leave here, though it may be conceit on my part to think I can help her better than the Walterses' family doctor . . .'

'It isn't,' Toni interrupted. 'You do help her, and chiefly in a spiritual way. Dr Price is an old man, set in his ways, and a complete materialist—even Father finds him a bit trying—and he wouldn't in the least understand Marcia. Dr Price, if he heard half of what we know, would treat her as a mental case, and she isn't, is she?'

'No—not in the accepted meaning of that word. I can only make the hackneyed quotation, which seems to suit her case so well: "There are more things in heaven and earth, than are dreamed of in your philosophy." '

'Would a priest be of any help to her?' Toni did not understand what induced her to ask the question.

'Not unless she wanted to see a priest.'

'But Marcia knows nothing of any religion, except what she picked up from Janet Cameron, and that didn't appeal to her. She told me so, but she said that when she went into the old churches in Paris and Spain she was soothed and happy.'

'Are you suggesting that I should try to convert Marcia?' inquired Richard, looking slightly amused.

'You wouldn't have to. She was baptized into the Catholic Faith when she was a baby.'

'How do you know that?'

'Alma told me. When those poor babies were born they were not expected to live. Mrs Norman had originally been a Catholic, and she had them baptized. She probably thought she owed them that, though no doubt she hoped they would die immediately afterwards. Alma herself told me that she was more than half inclined to speak to Father Arnon in Seacrest about Marcia, only he doesn't seem the type. He's old and feeble, and I really don't think he could cope with any problem outside the usual routine, though he's a dear old saint.'

'Nevertheless it would be a good idea to get in touch with him,' Richard said.

'Couldn't you sound Marcia, and discover her attitude?' Toni said. 'You will be seeing her tomorrow.'

'I must think about it, Toni.' And then Richard added with a smile: 'It's strange that you with your firm belief that all Churches are unnecessary should want to see Marcia brought back to the Church.'

'I think it's the right thing if a person needs a Church, and will get consolation through it.'

'But you wouldn't.'

'Oh, Richard, I don't know . . . but it seems so cowardly to rush to shelter just because one wants to be reassured and comforted and be looked after in a spiritual sense.'

'But that is just what the Church is—a shelter,' Richard said.

'But don't you admire the person who does good for the sake of doing good, who is strong enough to stand alone, who asks no quarter?'

'Yes, exactly as one can admire the old Roman gladiators—and pity them. Doing good is not less precious, but more so, if you do it for the love of God. You can be valiant within the Church, and you can stand up to quite a lot of things without asking quarter.'

She sighed. 'But surely even you must feel sometimes that Destiny or God is cruel. I don't mean only because of wars and famines and shipwrecks, and the way in which men torture one another. I know those things happen mainly through the evil of men themselves, but in the terrible fates which are meted out to the innocents, to children who are born imbeciles, or with congenital diseases . . . to children who are handicapped as Monica and Marcia were handicapped. What purpose can there be in such torture?'

'I don't know, Toni.'

'I dare say you think it's quite probable that Mrs Norman did bring a curse upon herself.'

'I believe nothing so ridiculous. I have no solution to these problems, except—that this life is no more than a prologue, important mainly because we can have no after-life without it.'

'I suppose you think that in the life after death everyone who has suffered unjustly here has it made up to them.'

'Well, why not? That's a logical aftermath if you believe in a just God. Darling, there is no human explanation for thousands of cruel undeserved wrongs, but then neither is there an explanation for thousands of undeserved joys.'

'I envy you your Faith in a personal God, but I'm one of those who ask for a sign. If one were given to me I wouldn't ignore it.'

'You may get your sign, Toni, though possibly you've been given dozens of signs and have ignored them. It must be an unsatisfactory thing to believe in a vague Supreme Being, yet you cling to it obstinately, don't you?'

'I suppose I do . . . not that I want to . . . it's unsatisfactory as you say, but my reasoning powers were given me for some purpose, and my heart and soul cannot accept what my reason denies.'

Richard smiled. 'Your reason,' he said, 'was given you to help you solve the problems of earthly existence, not to try to probe the Infinite.'

Toni moved pettishly. 'I knew we should come up upon the Infinite and the finite mind sooner or later . . . it's the one unassailable answer to every question.'

'It is indeed,' Richard agreed.

Toni looked at him with irritation and with envy and with affection. 'Well, there's a high wall, and I can't climb over it,' she said. 'It's a pity, isn't it?'

'Oh, I don't know . . . one day you'll possibly find there's no wall there at all . . . it will have melted away and perhaps sooner than you expect,' he said.

10

When Toni arrived at Meadow House that afternoon she was greeted by Alma. Wondering if Louis had given her an indication of his intention, Toni looked at her searchingly, but Alma seemed as usual, and almost at once said that

Louis had had a summons to London, difficult to disregard.

'He's becoming really important,' Alma said with pardonable pride. 'It's something when he's asked to be a speaker at a big dinner.'

'It is indeed,' Toni agreed. 'But then, as you said the other day, everything has gone smoothly for Louis. Few people, I imagine, make an immediate success.'

Alma looked rather guilty. 'I said some hard things of Louis. I was angry with him and afraid for Marcia. I thought he didn't understand her, and wasn't sufficiently understanding. But he was very sweet when he said goodbye to her today. He sat talking to her for quite a time and said she must get well quickly and what a shame it was that she couldn't come to London with him. I was most relieved.'

'You must have been,' Toni said. She scarcely knew what to make of Louis's duplicity. He might have forced himself to show kindness, but if he had convinced Marcia that all was well, it might make it harder for her in the future.

'I'm really glad he'll be away for a few days,' Alma went on. 'Cosmo Gallion's death, and finding out about Marcia and her twin has been a shock to him, and I doubt if men stand up to shocks as well as women. If he's away from Marcia for a little while he'll get a better perspective.'

'Perhaps he will,' said Toni, without much hope.

'Marcia's a darling, but I really do think she should have special treatment. If she stayed in a nursing home for a few weeks, she might come out a different person. After all, what do we know about the mind and its peculiarities?'

'Nothing at all,' Toni agreed. 'But I thought it was exorcism in which you put your trust.'

'Well, so it is, but I know Louis would never consent to it, neither can I imagine poor old Father Arnon having anything to do with it.'

'Have you mentioned this to Marcia?' Toni asked.

'Oh, yes, and she's willing to do anything, but of course she will expect Louis to make the decision.'

Toni wondered if Louis would be sufficiently interested.

It was not so much Marcia's delusions which worried him, as that she had been Monica's twin, joined to her in death as in life, and as he was convinced, malformed as much in personality as in body.

'By the way,' Alma went on, 'Marcia wants you to have tea with her alone in the studio. She asked me if she could have it there as a treat. She's arranging it all herself. I made some special cakes this morning and cut the sandwiches. She's quite excited—like a child—she has even dressed herself up for the occasion.'

'She didn't mind Louis leaving her, then?'

'Oh, no. As I told you he was sweet and understanding with her before he left, and I believe it's really a relief to her, as the separation is only for a short time.'

'Aren't you included in the tea-party?' Toni asked.

'No, dear. I shall go into Seacrest to do some shopping. You can manage without me, can't you? I shan't be gone longer than an hour, and Marcia is really quite well today.'

Toni saw Alma start off, and then went up the stairs to the studio. Since the house-party week-end, it had reverted to the room where Marcia could work and rest. It looked very attractive, Toni thought, for there were cream silk curtains, deep chairs and a small tea-table drawn up before a brightly blazing fire. Marcia's easel had been pushed up against the wall. Instead of working she was sitting in one of the big chairs, staring into the fire. As Toni came in she put out her hand in welcome.

'I'm glad you were free this afternoon. I wanted to talk to you. You went away so quickly after the lunch yesterday. I hadn't a chance to say a word to you.'

'You were worn out—you had had enough conversation,' Toni said.

'Oh, now you're speaking like a nurse, but as a matter of fact, I felt much better, once I had told everyone the sort of person I really am.'

'My dear, we all know the sort of person you really are. The person who has made us all love her.'

There was something odd about Marcia this afternoon, though Toni could not analyse it. Alma had spoken about her childishness, but she did not look at all childish. She was wearing a sophisticated dress which reminded Toni of the one she had worn on her first meeting with Cosmo Gallion. This of course was an afternoon dress, but it was black and cleverly cut, and made her look years older.

'Do you really love me, Toni?' As Marcia spoke, she glanced at the other in a sidelong way—a curious glance which seemed to measure her, to appraise her.

'You know I do. It's not difficult for you to win affection.'

'Even though I'm only half a person?'

'I don't agree with that . . . it's no more than a morbid idea. You are a complete person in yourself, responsible for yourself—you always were.'

'I used to tell myself so, but I don't know that I really believed it, and I'm perfectly sure that Louis doesn't believe it.'

Toni considered this for a moment in silence.

'I realize your difficulty,' she said, 'but if you care enough for Louis you will have patience. In time he will forget what happened when you were born. He will realize that it makes no difference, but you have to heal yourself first. You must realize that Monica is dead, and can no longer hurt you. She is far away in another world.'

'You think that, do you?'

Toni started. The sudden change in Marcia's voice was extraordinary. She laughed, a harsh and ugly laugh. Astounded, Toni stared at her. The fair and lovely face was altered. It was darker, the eyes had a wild, fierce expression, the mouth curved in a cruel sneer.

'What a fool you are,' Marcia said in that new, rough voice. 'Some people never die . . . they cling . . . they don't let go.'

Fear laid a frozen finger on Toni's heart. She was cold and yet she was stifled. The air was heavy and clogged her breath. She wanted to fling the windows wide open and then as she glanced across the room she saw that they were already open. Nevertheless the stifling sensation continued. While she still sat there speechless, Marcia said, 'Let's have a drink, before I make the tea. Which do you prefer, sherry or something stronger? A whisky?'

Toni thought that for once she could do with a strong drink, and accepted it.

Marcia moved across the room to a corner cupboard which, when opened, revealed various bottles. Watching her curiously, Toni thought she even walked differently, jerkily, almost clumsily. She came back to Toni with two glasses already filled. One she set down on the small table by Toni's side, and then stood leaning against the mantelpiece with her own glass in her hand. Before Toni could raise her glass to her lips the telephone bell rang, and as Marcia crossed to the instrument and took up the receiver, Toni said: 'I didn't know you had followed our example and had the telephone put in.'

'It's only recent. Alma thought it would be convenient for me. Oh, it's for you . . . it's Dr Carlyn.'

Toni got up, and with her glass in her hand, took the receiver from Marcia.

'What is it?' she asked anxiously. 'It's not Father . . . he's not worse?'

'Just as usual; I've only this minute left him,' came Richard's voice in reply. 'I rang up because for no reason on earth I suddenly felt worried about you. I wanted to be sure of your whereabouts.'

'But that's crazy, Richard,' and Toni laughed. 'You knew very well I should be here.'

'I knew you'd started for Meadow House—I wasn't sure you had got there.'

'Well, I really don't see what could have happened to me on a mile of country road practically devoid of traffic, but I know what these unreasoning presentiments are; you can't argue about them. Set your mind at rest, though, I'm perfectly all right. Goodbye for now, my dear.'

She hung up the receiver and walked back to Marcia.

'Richard seemed to think I might have been set upon by highwaymen on my way here,' she said, and then as Marcia did not reply, she gazed speculatively at the contents of her glass and raised it to her lips. The next instant the glass was knocked out of her hand. It fell to the ground and was smashed into a dozen fragments.

'Marcia!' Toni cried.

'I won't let you do it . . . I won't!' Marcia cried. 'I don't care . . . she's my friend . . . and even if she's not . . . I won't have anyone else killed.'

'You fool,' said another voice, a voice which was certainly not Marcia's. 'Through her you'll lose everything.'

Toni thought: 'I'm going mad—there's nobody here but Marcia and I, and yet I can hear someone else talking.'

She rubbed her eyes; a thick mist seemed to be blinding them . . . it was more than a mist, for wreaths of smoke filled the room, smoke which seemed to be forming a kind of pattern in the air, a pattern which gradually resolved itself into the uncertain outline of a human form.

She saw the thing gaining substance, saw the outline of a white dress, dark curls which fell heavily upon a woman's neck, a dark face rising up out of the mist, evil and furious with thwarted fury.

'It's over,' Marcia said. 'I'm stronger than you now, and I always will be stronger. It was through my weakness that you were able to be part of me . . . I was sorry and I loved you, and I let you in . . . but now it's over . . . I never will again . . .'

There was no sound of laughter, and yet Toni knew that the misty, half-formed creature was laughing. The voice said, 'You can't get rid of me . . . I'm part of yourself, the dead part, but there are those who help the dead . . .'

Marcia covered her face with her hands and sobbed, and for a moment it was as though she disappeared in the mist which swam floatingly between them. A dreadful sickness seized Toni—the air was so fetid and close that she could not breathe. Somehow she staggered to the door and tore it open. Fresh air streamed in to her from the open window on the landing, and as her legs gave way beneath her, she stumbled and fell.

She was conscious of nothing until she felt a hand laid on her shoulder and realized that Marcia was bending over her.

'It's all right,' Marcia said. 'She's gone.'

Her voice was hoarse as though with extreme exhaustion, and when Toni looked up at her and somehow got to her feet, it was evident that she was indeed exhausted. Her face was the colour of clay, and there were dark smudges beneath her eyes.

'I'm free of her now,' Marcia said, 'but I don't know for how long. I've won the battle this time, and I don't often. The strength goes out of her and she leaves me, but when her strength is renewed she comes back.'

She took Toni's hand and drew her back into the room. Toni looked around her, almost believing that the scene she had witnessed was some nightmare fantasy; the air was clear now, and the mild autumn breeze fluttered the curtains, but on the floor there were the fragments of broken glass and the dark patch where the liquid had soaked the carpet.

'I meant to kill you,' Marcia said. 'Or at least I suppose it was me . . . I'm so mixed up with Monica, that sometimes I hardly know which of us decides things. It was she who thought of it. I had a lot of sleeping stuff, and some of it was dangerous. A double dose would be enough to kill anyone. Alma had it hidden away in her room, but Monica knew where it was and she told me. I took the bottle, and emptied what was in it into another bottle, and then I filled the first bottle with water so that Alma shouldn't know. It hadn't much taste and I put some in your whisky . . . or was it Monica who did that? I can't remember.'

She put her hand to her forehead and swayed, and Toni forgetting herself, made her sit down in one of the big chairs.

'I suppose I was willing for her to do it, to be me for a little while today,' Marcia said. 'She made me believe that I wanted to kill you, but when I saw you—when I saw you starting to drink it . . . then I couldn't, I couldn't! Whatever you have done to me, Toni, I still love you.'

'But I've done nothing to hurt you,' said Toni. 'Nothing at all.'

'Louis loves you,' said Marcia.

Instinctively and immediately Toni lied. 'What can have put that idea into your head? Of course he does not.'

'I heard him when he spoke to you on the telephone last

night. He thought I was asleep, but I wasn't. I followed him down the stairs, and I stood in the bend of the staircase and I heard him. He never knew I was there. I heard him say he had made a ghastly mistake, that he felt as though he had been dragged into a bog . . . that all he said to you before he went to Spain was still true. I got back to my room without Louis seeing me, for after he had spoken to you he went into the library.'

Toni said, 'You can't condemn people by the evidence of a telephone conversation. I agree that Louis was very overwrought, bewildered and upset. He was resentful because all his life had become chaotic. I am an old friend, and he knew he could trust me, he turned to me for comfort. But he doesn't love me and never has.'

She lied without compunction, knowing that she could do nothing else, and with relief she saw Marcia relax, saw something of trust and hope come back into her eyes. But then the tears started to roll down her cheeks.

'Oh, Toni, if you had drunk that stuff, it would have killed you,' she said.

Toni shook her head and answered cheerfully, 'I don't suppose it would. I should probably have slept for hours; that's all.'

There was a long pause before Marcia said, 'You saw her, didn't you?'

'Yes, I saw her.' Toni could not repress a shudder.

'And you know that everything I said was true. Just now I told her I was stronger than she, and that she would never be able to come back, but I know it isn't true. She changes me . . . she wants me to do terrible things . . . and yet she loves me. How can I really hate her? There's nothing I can do, nothing. I shall never be free.'

'Marcia, you shall be . . . there must be a way, but I have to think.'

'I've tried everything. I've prayed to her . . . and she would do most things for me. But that one thing, she won't do. I was never meant to leave her, she says, and I never shall. Yet though she's jealous of me, in a way she wants me to be happy: for she tried to get rid of you because you might take Louis from me.'

Toni said thoughtfully, 'It would be better to pray to God than to pray to her. He is the only one who can help you.'

'But perhaps God meant it to be this way.'

'Oh no, oh no, you mustn't think that . . . you have to fight, darling, and all we who love you must help you to fight.'

Marcia leant back with a deep and exhausted sigh.

'It's something to know that you really believe me at last, that you don't think I'm mad.'

Toni observed her with concern. She had never been so conscious of Marcia's physical fragility. Her slender arms were wasted and her skin had a transparent quality.

'I could die,' Marcia went on in her weak voice, 'but I'm afraid, not of death itself, but of being joined to her again. The only thing I can do is to go right away somewhere . . . live in some remote place and . . . and welcome Monica, let her stay with me, and be part of me.'

'Oh no, no,' Toni cried in horror.

An agonizing compassion tore at her. Never as long as she lived would she forget the terrible sense of contact with absolute evil, and to think of Marcia voluntarily opening her heart and soul, giving it permission to live within her, was appalling.

'Marcia,' she said suddenly, 'I know you don't practise any formal religion, but when you were a baby you were baptized into the Catholic Church, and so you still are a Catholic. That being so, would you consent to see a priest?'

'But what good would it do?' Marcia asked.

'I think it might help. You would be dealing then with someone versed in spiritual matters. There's just a chance that you might be delivered from this torment.'

'If that were possible, I would do anything,' Marcia said.

She was so tired now that she could scarcely speak, and Toni said gently, 'I shall help you to bed, and then when Alma comes I shall go home . . . and don't despair, you will be all right for tonight I think. But fight, Marcia . . . do fight . . . every time you give way it must increase her strength.'

'I'll try,' Marcia said faintly. 'If only I didn't feel so battered. Oh Toni, say you forgive me for what I tried to do!'

Toni had walked over to Meadow House and so had to walk back again, but she had not gone more than a quarter of a mile before she met Richard.

'Did you come to find me?' she asked.

'Yes, even after our telephone conversation I felt fidgety about you, unable to get you out of my mind, even for five minutes.'

Toni said, 'Actually I was in some danger this afternoon.'

'You were?' He looked at her closely.

She proceeded to give him an account of all that had happened during the last hour, though uncertain as to whether he would believe her. When put into words it was the most extraordinary story, and she was convinced she told it badly and unconvincingly. But Richard listened in silence and then said, 'So you did get your sign, though not in any pleasant form.'

This startled her. 'You mean that now convinced of the reality of absolute evil, it follows that I must also be convinced of the reality of absolute goodness?'

'Isn't that your own conclusion?'

'Yes, I suppose it is.'

'Then, my darling, I think it was almost worth your terrifying experience and the risk you ran of being poisoned.'

'Would it have poisoned me? I made light of it to Marcia, pretended it would only have sent me into a doped sleep.'

'You ran a grave risk. Something will have to be done about this, you know. It's too dangerous to be allowed to continue.'

Toni cried out in alarm. 'For heaven's sake, you wouldn't think of having her put in a home?'

'Not unless all other methods fail, but she may have to have a permanent nurse-companion. However, I'm inclined to see Father Arnon first, and have a word with him. I'm glad you spoke of that to Marcia—at least she will be willing to see him.'

'Do you think the Church can help her?'

'I have hope, Toni, and if I call on Father Arnon this evening, he may be able to visit Marcia tomorrow. It's just as well that Louis is away. He might be obstructive.'

'Yes, he might, but Alma will welcome help of any kind. I'll show you Father Arnon's house, and I'll wait for you, or drop in to see a friend for half an hour. I don't want to have to tell that story all over again, Richard . . . you can tell it for me.'

To this Richard agreed, and they continued their walk in silence. Toni was conscious of feeling desperately tired. Just before they left for Seacrest Alma rang up. She was not too happy about Marcia, she told Toni. She was restless, was unable to sleep, and had been wandering about the house for the last hour in a distracted condition.

Alma knew nothing of the events of that afternoon, for Toni had had no opportunity to tell her, but she said worriedly that she had never known Marcia to be in a more agitated mood. Probably Louis's absence had something to do with it.

Toni said reassuringly that Richard would call in to see Marcia some time that evening. They were going to Seacrest on business, and would stop at Meadow House on their homeward way.

Repeating this conversation to Richard, Toni said, 'I don't know why I didn't tell her the truth—that you were going to see Father Arnon about Marcia, except—well, I could be afraid that he won't be interested.'

'He'll be interested,' Richard said, 'but there's the chance that we may not find him in. We ought to have telephoned for an appointment.'

However, when they reached the priest's house, and the door was opened to them by an elderly woman housekeeper, they were told that Father Arnon was at supper but would see them in a few minutes.

'See him by yourself, please, Richard,' Toni said, as they sat in the small stiffly furnished room. 'I didn't intend to come in, but perhaps it's just as well I should be here, for if necessary I can tell him of my experience.'

The housekeeper returned as she spoke, and said that the Father was ready to see them, and Richard left Toni alone. She waited for over three-quarters of an hour, and never had time passed more slowly for her. At last the door opened and Richard came in, followed by the old priest.

Father Arnon was over seventy, he was tall, spare, grey-haired. His eyes were gentle and visionary, his smile benign. When he had been introduced to Toni and had greeted her, he said, 'Dr Carlyn tells me that you can support what he has told me. It's a strange story, but I have heard many strange stories. Obviously it is my duty to help this poor girl in any way I can.'

'Father Arnon wants to see Marcia at once,' Richard explained to Toni. 'He's prepared to return with us, now.'

'Shouldn't we telephone Alma and prepare her?' Toni asked.

'I don't think it's necessary. You have already told her that we shall be calling on our homeward way.'

Toni said no more, except to apologize to Father Arnon, who was bound to be uncomfortable in the small pony cart intended only for two. When they pulled up outside Meadow House, they saw there were lights in many of the rooms, and when Alma opened the door to them, it was evident that she was thankful to see them.

'What a dreadful evening,' she cried, clutching Toni's arm. 'Most people would say that Marcia is completely out of her mind, but I know, I know she isn't. It has been terrible to see . . . she has gone from one fit to another—if fits they are. She has been incredibly brave, and she has fought until she's exhausted.'

Toni said, 'Father Arnon is here, Alma. He thinks he may be able to help Marcia. Richard has told him about her.'

'I'm glad . . . I'm thankful.' Alma stretched out her hand to the priest.

'Where is she now?' Richard asked.

'In her room. I've only just managed to get her there. She's been all over the house, poor child . . . struggling, wrestling. I turned on all the lights, it was too horrible in the dark. Again and again she cried out: "No—no, I'll never let you in," and at last she fell down unconscious. Dr Carlyn, I saw that dreadful creature, I did indeed . . . she looked as solid, as real as you or I, and then when Marcia denied her she started to fade. I was afraid Marcia would die before you got here . . . I'd say she has endured as much as a human being can endure, and it was terrible to be alone with her.'

Father Arnon spoke for the first time. 'Please take me to her,' he said.

As he and Richard went up the stairs together, Alma collapsed weeping in Toni's arms. There was a short space of complete silence, and then they heard a piercing cry, and Marcia in a night-gown and a thin wrapper, with her hair dishevelled, her face dark and congested, appeared at the top of the stairs.

'Oh Alma, Alma,' she wailed, 'I've got to give in . . . I've got to.'

She gazed blankly at Richard as though she did not know him, and then her eyes fell on Father Arnon. It was a long, asking, pleading gaze, while tears streamed down her cheeks. Slowly she moved towards him.

Toni pulled Alma with her into the drawing-room and closed the door.

Time passed and Alma and Toni sat in silence. Once Alma started up, as she heard a door open. Then she sank back in her chair and said, 'It's only Hetty coming in—that was the back door. She'll go up to bed, and I hope will never know what has happened here tonight.'

The hands of the clock moved slowly. An hour passed and still that uncanny silence persisted. Neither of them could attempt ordinary conversation, but presently Toni suggested making tea, and Alma assented.

Hetty had long since retired, and in the empty kitchen Toni, who knew where to find what she required, arranged a tea-tray, and was thus occupied when she heard Richard descend the stairs. He came into the kitchen and stood leaning against the wall, watching her.

'How—how is she?' Toni asked, and was trembling as she spoke.

'At peace—now. Father Arnon will be down in a few

minutes. Don't ask me any questions, please. Even to you I could not describe what I have seen tonight. That simple old man . . . he's a saint . . . and Marcia is one of the bravest women I have ever known. She gave us all the help she could, but it has nearly finished her . . . physically. You must be prepared for that.'

'Did Father Arnon succeed in . . . in what you hoped he could do? I must ask you that much.'

'He succeeded. In that way I am sure Marcia will not be troubled again.'

Toni looked with pity at his white and exhausted face. She said, 'Go in to Alma. The kettle is boiling and I will make tea.'

By the time she carried the tray to the drawing-room, Father Arnon had joined them. He sat in the big chair by the fire, looking so frail, so utterly spent that Toni was frightened for him. He took the cup of tea from her and drank it. He said gently, when Alma ventured to question him, that they should all pray in gratitude that night because of Marcia's deliverance.

The evil being which had tortured her had been finally defeated, and had gone to its own place. She would be troubled with it no more. He would call tomorrow to see Marcia, and would do so every day while she lived.

Toni turned her frightened eyes upon Richard.

'Does that mean she is dying?' she asked.

'I'm afraid so, my dear,' he said. 'I told you her heart was weak; several times this evening, I thought it was all over for her.'

Alma broke into bitter weeping. 'It's as though that other one--the dead twin was half her strength,' she sobbed. 'Marcia's life has been sacrificed.'

'But not her soul,' Father Arnon said gently. 'Her soul is safe for evermore.'

A strange, smooth sense of peace stole over Toni's heart. She sat very still, allowing the benediction of it to possess her spirit.

II

Alma telephoned Louis the next day, urging him to come home as soon as possible, owing to Marcia's state of health. Possibly this was not taken as seriously as Alma intended, for he did not leave until after the literary dinner party, which took place the following evening.

By that time Marcia was so weak that she had ceased to ask for him, ceased to speak.

Toni, when she first saw her, had been horrified by the change in her. It was as though in a few hours the flesh had been literally stripped from her bones. She lay propped up with pillows, her emaciated arms lying on each side of her, her thin hands so weak that she could scarcely lift them. There were deep hollows in her cheeks, and her eyes looked enormous, but her expression was one of extraordinary peace and happiness.

A hospital nurse had been engaged, a pleasant-faced girl who, as Alma said, gave the minimum of trouble in the house. In any case it was obvious that she would be needed for only a few days.

Marcia was slipping away fast, but easily and without rebellion or regret. Holding Toni's hand, she said in her soft, whispering voice, 'I'm so terribly happy. It's so wonderful to be alone at last . . . poor Monica, she knows now that she is a separate person. She can never come back here any more, but there's hope for her. I know there's hope, for how could she help being born as she was?'

'Don't think of her, darling, think of yourself . . . try to get well,' Toni said, for it seemed to her that if that other miracle had been achieved, the miracle of giving life and health back to Marcia was also possible.

Marcia shook her head. 'That's not required of me. It's

time for me to go—and I'm not sorry, Toni. I've lost Louis's love, and I couldn't bear it if I had to get well again.'

She went on to speak of The Red Towers. She wanted to make a new Will, leaving enough to support the home, and the rest of her money to Louis. She was strong enough to give instructions to the lawyer who would be over that afternoon to see her, strong enough to sign her name to the document. During the next two or three days Father Arnon was much at the house, and was alone with Marcia for long periods. That he could give her comfort and reassurance was not to be doubted. No human being could have feared death less, nor have suffered less during those last days which, to Toni, would always be remembered as days of shining happiness.

Yet Marcia said little, asked for nothing, did not apparently speculate as to what was to be her fate in another world. Her attitude, Tony realized, was one of complete trust and acceptance. She had been cruelly victimized, but she had been miraculously delivered—that was enough for the dying Marcia, and Toni supposed that under the same circumstances it would also have been enough for her.

By the time Louis arrived, Marcia was beyond speech, and even beyond recognition of him.

Toni, sadly clear-sighted now where Louis was concerned, was sure this was a relief to him. The shrunken girl in the bed, with her small face as white as the pillows, still and unconscious, had little resemblance to the radiant, strangely fascinating girl he had married. For the sake of convention he could assume the proper degree of grief, but he felt none. Yet Toni was not unaware of his bewildered distress. He had loved so wildly only a few months ago, but now when he looked back upon that time, it had a dreamlike unreality.

The haunted girl of the last few weeks was much more real to him than the enchanting creature he had first met in Spain, and for her he felt only a chilled aversion.

So it was that Marcia died, peacefully and without pain; died in her sleep, for during that last day she did not once open her eyes.

Looking down at her as she lay there smiling, with flowers in her hands, it was impossible for Toni to grieve, she could only be glad that the way had been made so easy for Marcia, that she had escaped so much.

'I wish I could feel it was a terrible loss to me, but I can't,' Louis said. 'It was the best thing for Marcia too. My mother talked of medical treatment, but in our hearts we all know that sooner or later she would have had to be put away in a home.'

It was the day after the funeral, and as Alma was in bed, ill and worn out with shock and grief, Toni had called round to see her. She had been about to leave the house, had opened the front door, when Louis had waylaid her.

Toni would gladly have escaped, but without very plain speaking this would have been impossible, and therefore she resigned herself to the painful half-hour which Louis was determined to force on her. That their conversation should last no longer, she was resolved.

'I'm not a conventional person and neither are you,' Louis said desperately, when he had closed the study door, and Toni with a sigh had dropped down into a chair, prepared to give him her attention. 'I know this is too early to speak, but I can't endure you to think badly of me, and I feel it's only fair that I should be allowed to vindicate myself.'

'But why should you?' Toni said. 'You made yourself clear when we last saw each other. The fact that Marcia was a conjoined twin so revolted you that you couldn't tolerate her as a wife. Nobody can help those strong aversions. You decided to go away for a time, which was probably the best thing you could do. Alma says that you and Marcia parted affectionately, and she had no idea you planned to make a final break. You have nothing with which to reproach yourself.'

'Well—no, I haven't—really—and I certainly did not realize, when Mother telephoned me, that Marcia was likely to die within forty-eight hours; otherwise I should have forgone that dinner. I came immediately afterwards.'

'Alma couldn't bear to give you too great a shock,' Toni said. 'But Marcia was happy—it didn't matter that you weren't there—she had given up all her earthly affections, and had found something better to take their place.'

Louis stared at her coldly. He said, 'To hear you, one might think that you had "got religion"!'

'Perhaps I have. Has your mother told you about what happened here the night you left?'

'Oh yes, some fantastic story . . . I can't say it greatly impressed me, but then I've never taken your view that Marcia was diabolically possessed. You and Mother both hypnotized yourself into that belief, and then you roped in this Father Arnon who is probably a natural mystic and between you, you staged a kind of revivalist meeting —ably abetted by your precious Richard Carlyn.'

'It wasn't like that,' Toni said. 'But I dare say it's easier for you to believe it was. Actually Alma and I were not present when Father Arnon exorcized Monica's spirit, and Richard wasn't there all the time—he stayed outside her room. But she was a free soul when she died, Louis.'

He shrugged. 'Oh well, have it your own way. Mine is the unpopular view, as I well realize. Marcia, born as she was, was as deformed mentally as she was physically. She was beautiful and I fell in love with her, and was rushed into marriage by Janet Cameron who unscrupulously deceived me. When I began to fathom the sort of girl I had married, realized that she was abnormal, I fell out of love with her and who can blame me?'

'Nobody does blame you, Louis—only yourself,' Toni said gently.

A startled expression flashed into his eyes, and then to her dismay she saw his face quiver and crumple up in a grief and pain which stabbed her heart. He sat down at his desk and covered his face with his hands.

'Oh, my dear,' Toni said, and went to him.

He grasped her hand and dragged it to his lips.

'Toni . . . try to understand. It was a mad thing—it ought never to have happened, but I'm sorry—sorry . . .'

'Yes, I know you are,' she soothed, 'and wherever Marcia is she knows it too. Don't think she considered herself blameless. She did deceive you. She took that risk with her eyes open.'

'She was so young,' Louis grieved, 'so beautiful—and all her life wasted. She had less than a year of real life.'

'It wasn't wasted. In the end she knew that—she was sure that she had not suffered in vain, and Louis, there is still much that you can do for her.'

'Don't tell me I can pray for her soul.' His voice broke on the sneer.

'I wasn't thinking of prayers, but she wanted to help the poor and the sick. She has left enough money to keep the Home going, and if you would take a personal interest in it, perhaps give part of the money she has left to you, to supplement her gift, it might be of the greatest consolation to you. If you were cruel to her, it would be atonement.'

He did not answer at once, though he pressed her hand closely. At last he said, 'You're the dearest girl . . . What a fool I've been, for once I could have had all your sweetness for myself.'

The renunciation in his voice was sincere and Toni drew an inaudible breath of relief. She said, 'We shouldn't have been happy . . . we have both turned away from the love we thought we had for one another. You turned to Marcia, and I love Richard Carlyn.'

He groaned. 'I knew that before you said it.'

'I have to love him, Louis, he's so good, so dear—I understand him so well. I know we shall be happy.'

'You'll probably kill yourself for him. You'll work in that noisome slum, bear him children, share his arrogant, demanding religion.'

Toni uttered a soft laugh. 'Yes, I suppose it is arrogant in a heavenly sort of way, and it's certainly demanding. I'm glad of that . . . I wouldn't have it otherwise. I hope yours is a true prophecy, my dear . . . my poor dear . . .'

'Then if that is what you want, my darling, it means goodbye.'

'Not to friendship, Louis.'

'Friendship is not the kind of thing I want from you,'

he said, and Toni smiled, remembering how, a few months ago, when he had returned to Meadow House with his bride, he would have been aghast had she demanded anything else. She said, 'I must go now, Louis, but don't forget about The Red Towers. You can help to make something great of it, if you will.'

'I'll think it over,' he said, and with that she had to be content.

Richard was on the point of leaving, and he was sitting with Everard Benham when Toni returned. She was rushed and out of breath and said apologetically, 'I knew I was cutting it very fine, but they were upset over there, and I couldn't get away sooner.'

Richard said, 'I suppose you really mean that you couldn't get away from Louis Walters.'

'Yes—well, I had to stay. He was wretched, poor soul. He blames himself for a lot, but he insists that he doesn't. I suggested that he could come to terms with himself by doing all he could for the convalescent home, to which Marcia has left so much of her money.' And then, as Richard was silent, Toni added: 'Louis told me that I was fated to marry you, to bear you children, and slave for you in your filthy slum district and embrace your arrogant and demanding creed.'

Richard turned to look at her. 'He did, did he? And what did you say to that?'

'I said I hoped his prophecy would come true.'

There was a long moment of silence, and then Richard reached for her, clasped his arms round her, pulled her to him.

'Oh, darling . . . darling,' he muttered.

She said, when at last he released her, 'But we shall have to wait, Richard. I can't leave Father, and as for the religion part—I couldn't rush into it.'

'I wouldn't ask it of you.'

'But I do believe—with all my heart. I can't bear to think that Marcia had to suffer so much to benefit others, and yet there's no doubt that she changed the world for me through what she endured.'

'It's just a dim view of a tiny piece of tapestry,' Richard said.

'What do you mean?'

'That's the way I often see life, as a closely woven pattern that none of us can possibly understand. It seems brutal that Marcia was in bondage, and yet she will probably count herself blessed because that was the fate mapped out for her—just her minute part of the design. She didn't puzzle over things at the end you know, she bore no resentment, she only accepted—was glad to accept.'

Happy in her lover's arms. Toni yet sighed deeply. 'Shall I ever be like that, I wonder?' she said. 'It's my instinct to rebel, to want to put things right.'

'And so you shall—you shall order my life for me and boss our children, and make me cringe before you,' Richard said.

But, laughing, she clung to him.

'Never, never . . . I shall spoil you. You need it . . . I'm going to ruin you with kindness and devotion,' she promised him.

Galien Township Library

Galien, Michigan

1. Books may be kept two weeks and may be renewed once for the same period, except 7 day books and magazines.

2. A fine is charged for each day a book is not returned according to the above rule. No book will be issued to any person incurring such a fine until it has been paid.

3. All injuries to books beyond reasonable wear and all losses shall be made good to the satisfaction of the Librarian.

4. Each borrower is held responsible for all books charged on his card and for all fines accruing on the same.